Valentine Flings

An affair to mend their broken hearts?

When nurse Ally signs herself and her best friend, GP Larissa, up for a posting with global charity New Health Frontiers, the idea is that they both see a bit of the world and hopefully find a little fun along the way!

After all, both women are nursing heartbreaks that have held them back from embracing life to the fullest, and as their assignments will put them in some far-flung locations at the most romantic time of the year, they decide to up the ante and dare each other to embark on a no-strings affair while away!

But they both find much more than they were expecting when their flings have the potential to turn from a bit of fun into happily-ever-after...

Indulge in Larissa and Erik's story in *Hot Nights with the Arctic Doc* by Luana DaRosa

And fall for Ally and Dev in *Nurse's Keralan Temptation* by Becky Wicks

Both available now!

T0284588

Dear Reader,

It was the start of a new era, working on this fun Valentine Flings duet with the wonderful Luana DaRosa. We must have spent hours on calls and WhatsApp, plotting the things our two like-minded friends were going to do to support each other in these stories. It was a lot of fun matching it all up. So much fun that we're going to write more together—watch this space!

I hope you enjoy this story, and Luana's, with appropriate sprinkles of sunshine and ice, and lots of love in between.

Becky x

NURSE'S KERALAN TEMPTATION

BECKY WICKS

MEDICAL ROMANCE

Harlequin®
MEDICAL ROMANCE

Recycling programs
for this product may
not exist in your area.

ISBN-13: 978-1-335-94281-4

Nurse's Keralan Temptation

Harlequin Enterprises ULC
22 Adelaide St. West, 41st Floor
Toronto, Ontario M5H 4E3, Canada
www.Harlequin.com

Printed in U.S.A.

Born in the UK, **Becky Wicks** has suffered interminable wanderlust from an early age. She's lived and worked all over the world, from London to Dubai, Sydney, Bali, New York City and Amsterdam. She's written for the likes of *GQ*, *Hello!*, *Fabulous* and *Time Out*, and has written a host of YA romance, plus three travel memoirs—*Burqalicious*, *Balilicious* and *Latinalicious* (HarperCollins, Australia). Now she blends travel with romance for Harlequin and loves every minute! Find her on Substack: @beckywicks.

Books by Becky Wicks

Harlequin Medical Romance

Falling Again for the Animal Whisperer
Fling with the Children's Heart Doctor
White Christmas with Her Millionaire Doc
A Princess in Naples
The Vet's Escape to Paradise
Highland Fling with Her Best Friend
South African Escape to Heal Her
Finding Forever with the Single Dad
Melting the Surgeon's Heart
A Marriage Healed in Hawaii
Tempted by the Outback Vet

Buenos Aires Docs

Daring to Fall for the Single Dad

Visit the Author Profile page
at Harlequin.com for more titles.

Dedicated to Simon, Charley and the cats.

CHAPTER ONE

ALLY SWIPED THE mounting beads of sweat from her forehead, dragging her giant suitcase behind her through arrivals. Its front wheel hadn't been broken at Heathrow, but someone had obviously tossed it too hard onto the plane. Of course, her bag would embarrass her now, careening all around her like an obstinate shopping trolley.

'Where is she?' she muttered to herself, scanning the bustling crowd. Dr Anjali Kapur—the Indian physician who would soon be assigning her tasks on her two-month assignment with New Health Frontiers was supposed to be here to meet her.

Pulling to a stop by a vending machine, she fanned out her shirt at the neck, praying she wouldn't be stranded here. It was already a thousand degrees. Well, OK, maybe only twenty-eight, but the sweltering humidity of Kerala was so far a stark contrast to the cold and rainy home she'd left behind in Somerset.

'Alison Spencer?' A melodic voice called out

from across the throng. Ally turned to see a striking woman with warm brown eyes and a big,
welcoming smile heading towards her, waving a
sign with her name on it that she had completely
missed. For a qualified nurse she wasn't all that
observant on the other end of the fifteen-hour
flight from the UK to southern India. The four-
hour layover in Doha hadn't helped. Due to a lack
of seating, she'd flopped in a shisha lounge and
politely declined offers from about three hopeful businessmen to indulge in a bubblegum-
flavoured smoke-fest.

'Dr Kapur? Hi! Yes, I'm Ally.' Ally reached
out for a sweaty handshake, which Anjali returned with a firm grip. Gosh, this woman was
strong, she thought. And really quite striking in
her fuchsia-pink lipstick. Anjali had the kind of
thick black luscious hair usually seen in TikTok
videos about hair-curling devices, and Ally was
suddenly more than conscious of her own un-
brushed auburn locks.

'Welcome to Kerala, Ally. Let's get you to
base. The team can't wait to meet you.'

They walked together towards the car park.
Ally couldn't help but admire Anjali's traditional
Indian attire. The vibrant colours of her sari were
mesmerising and almost seemed to dance around
her with each step she took. In contrast, Ally
felt painfully aware of her own 'very English'

clothes—practical and plain, jeans and a white shirt, both now sticking uncomfortably to her skin in the heat.

'The weather can take some getting used to,' Anjali remarked, seeing her mop at her brow with the back of her hand. 'But don't worry, you'll adapt soon enough.'

'Thanks for the reassurance,' Ally replied with a wry smile, already imagining what colour sari she might buy, as soon as she located a market. She also couldn't help but wonder how Larissa was getting on, and bit back a laugh just imagining it. Larissa—or Larry as she liked to call her, seeing as it made them rhyme—had taken a similar assignment with New Health Frontiers, only in Svalbard, a Norwegian archipelago stuck like a fractured iceberg between mainland Norway and the North Pole. Calling it 'out of her comfort zone' didn't cut it.

'Ready for the drive to HQ?' Anjali asked as they approached the car. 'We have air conditioning.'

'Oh, that's music to my ears,' Ally responded, her worry momentarily put aside. She'd already decided that whatever challenges lay ahead she would face them head-on, just as she had done back home in Frome for her sister, Nora, and Oliver, and for herself. Or tried to, at least. After two years in the UK without so much as a week-end escape, she deserved this. She was owed the chance to do something different for herself, but it wasn't as though she didn't feel guilty at the same time. Nora couldn't go far, what with Oliver being in school, but she had been very encouraging about this opportunity, saying it was time at least one of them took some time out after what had happened. They'd helped each other out of the pit of grief after Matt and Albie died, leaving Nora a widow, Oliver without a dad, and herself without the most loving, loyal boyfriend she'd ever had.

Nora had said it would do her good to 'get out there and do something different'. So she'd agreed and dragged Larry along too. Well, to their respective placements in totally different places. Who knew what else they would've done anyway, after the clinic boarded up its doors? Five years of working there together. Five years of making it all but their second home and building a practice that their clients trusted. While Larry always had a Plan B, C, D and E to fall back on, the future without Matt had stretched out ahead of Ally as empty as the pizza box after their final staff party.

The drive to the NHF headquarters took roughly an hour. Ally struggled to make polite conversation when all she wanted to do was sleep.

She couldn't help but think of Matt, either. He'd have liked it here. He'd wanted to visit India.

Two years…just over two years…since he and Albie took the boat out on what was meant to be the holiday of a lifetime in Sicily. Two years since she and Nora watched their boyfriend and husband respectively sail off on their lads' fishing trip. Two years since they discovered the boat had flipped, and their men were never coming home again.

Don't go there, Ally. You're here to focus on work.

Palm trees hung over the car most of the way. Horses and carts spoke of a life that was still semi-stuck somewhere in the eighteen hundreds, and the twinkling ocean, rising hills and vast watery landscapes soothed her mind at least.

The HQ building was much bigger than the local clinic she had worked at in Frome. It was modern and sleek, and it really stood out amongst the bustling city streets. Impressive, she thought. However, the moment she stepped through the doors of the New Health Frontiers headquarters, she got the distinct impression she'd just entered an entirely different world. The bustling facility was alive with sounds of people speaking multiple languages and the faint smell of disinfectant that reminded her of an overcrowded hospital. Medical supplies were stacked high on shelves, creating a maze through which staff seemed to navigate perfectly well despite the heat. Outside, Jeeps lined up like soldiers ready for their next mission.

'Everyone, this is Ally Spencer, our new community health nurse from England, who'll be with us till the end of February,' Anjali announced, leading Ally towards a group huddled around a table strewn with maps and documents. The small crowd looked up, offering welcoming nods and smiles, which she reciprocated.

'Meet Sameer, our logistics coordinator,' Anjali continued, pointing to a young man with a thick beard and round glasses. 'He makes sure everything runs smoothly.'

'Nice to meet you, Ally,' Sameer said warmly, extending his hand.

'This is Lila, our pharmacist,' Anjali continued. 'And Priya, one of our local translators.'

Ally followed behind Anjali, trying to memorise each person's name as they were introduced to her. There were actually more than her jet-lagged brain could handle. Dr Singh—head physician; Aryan—medical assistant; Rani—community outreach coordinator; Malik—lab technician… The list went on until, finally, Ally decided she would probably have to ask people to wear name badges the whole time, wherever she ended up. Still, as they walked through the headquarters, she soon felt excitement win out over her trepidation.

'Ah, yes. Ally, there's someone else I'd like you to meet,' Anjali said suddenly, stopping in front of a tall, striking, dark-skinned man who seemed to have appeared out of nowhere. Time ceased to tick as Ally took in his lean, muscular build and neat, short dark hair. His intense brown eyes conveyed a quiet intelligence that sucked her straight into some kind of vortex as he caught her gaze.

'Ally, this is Dev Chandran, one of our emergency medicine doctors,' Anjali introduced him with a smile. 'Dev, meet Ally Spencer.'

'Hi, Ally.' Dev extended his hand. 'Welcome to Kerala.'

He looked Indian himself, she thought, making a mental note of how his shirt was buttoned all the way to the top, as if he were afraid that people might forget to look him in the eyes if he revealed any more of that smooth, delicious mocha skin. Studious, yet sexy. And buff, too. When he wasn't being an emergency medic, she could tell he spent his time fending off wild elephants, flying over skyscrapers on motorbikes and sweeping women up in those sexy big brown arms. He looked good in those glasses too. *Good Lord*, this jet lag was kicking in hard.

'Hey, Dev,' she replied, trying to keep her voice steady as she shook his hand. His grip was firm, and something about the way he flashed a row of dazzling white teeth as he held her gaze made her heart race. He looked Indian sure enough, but did she detect an American accent? Canadian?

'Ally?' Dr Anjali Kapur's voice broke through her thoughts, and Ally blinked, realising she had been staring at Dev for quite a bit longer than was socially acceptable.

'Sorry,' she murmured, cheeks burning with embarrassment. She mumbled something about jet lag, wishing she had looked a bit nicer for these introductions.

'You must be tired,' Anjali replied, her tone gentle. 'It's been a long day already, and you've only just arrived.'

'Right.' Ally nodded, trying to focus on what her new colleague was saying. Dev was distracting her, and he wasn't even doing anything, just standing there looking great, looking at his phone. He frowned slightly as he read something and a line appeared in the middle of his forehead before he shoved it back into his pocket a little too hard. 'So, what's our assignment?' he asked now. 'You said Ally and I were on the first one together?'

Oh?

'Ah, yes,' Anjali began, turning to her. 'You and Dev will be leading a two-week measles and rubella vaccination drive together in the Way-anad District.'

'Is that close by?' she asked hopefully, picturing a shopping trip to the market for something a little less suffocating to wear.

'No, it's pretty remote. You'll be living together in a modest camp for the first two weeks, working very closely in a small team. All experienced NHFers.'

'Sounds like an adventure.' Ally tried to sound enthusiastic because it actually did sound like an adventure, but the words 'modest camp' were a red flag. Still, at least she would get two weeks with Dev and his preppy shirts and muscles. Maybe he could even be her 'fun fling'. She bit back a smile at the dare she'd made with Larissa. They were both supposed to have a fun fling in their prospective placements—something juicy that they could discuss together over long-distance calls. Really, she'd suggested it more for Larry's benefit. Larry had been a bit down lately, following that messy break-up with Rachel.

Following Matt's death, Ally hadn't exactly been the centre of anyone's attention, nor had she wanted to be, especially not romantically. She hadn't even dated anyone else, and why would she have? Not only had she been grieving the loss of a loving three-year relationship with the man she swore she would have married, had he asked, she'd seen Nora's total and utter devastation, having been widowed at thirty-seven years old. Her sister and Albie had been married for only three years…she'd met Matt at their wedding!

It was all enough to put her off relationships for life. And yet, here she was, undeniably attracted to the drool-worthy Dev Chandran. Ugh. Well, no harm in a crush, she supposed. It wasn't likely to go anywhere, not with them living 'modestly' on a campsite for the next two weeks, and after that, who knew where she'd be sent elsewhere in the country?

Dr Kapur excused herself, telling them their Jeep was ready when they were. Ally offered a grateful smile as the physician walked away. Oh, so they *were* going *right* now? Dev must have caught her look of panic.

'She likes us to get straight into it,' he explained. 'You can shower when we get there. Shall we?' He gestured towards the exit, where one of the Jeeps was waiting to take them on their journey into wherever the Wayanad District was.

The car ride to the remote village was another flurry of vivid colours and bustling activity that whizzed by as Ally sat in the back seat beside Dev. She tried to take it all in as the scenery grew more expansive and hilly and remote, but her mind kept drifting back to that electric moment when Dev's dark eyes had met hers. That had been quite shocking, all things considered. She hadn't been aware she could still be surprised like that, or feel butterflies like that. Maybe she had been imagining it though. She was so tired.

'Your first time in India?' Dev's warm voice pulled her out of her reverie.

'Yes,' Ally said, fighting back another yawn. 'It's quite different from Frome, that's for sure.'

'Frome? That sounds…cosy.'

'Does it? Well, if you like being stuck inside when it rains all the time, I suppose it is,' she agreed. 'How about you? Where are you from?'

'Toronto, originally. My parents came over from Mumbai for my father's work before we were born,' Dev said, adjusting his glasses on his nose and leaning back in the seat. 'I've been all over the place with NHF.'

'Wow,' Ally breathed, genuinely impressed. 'You must have some incredible stories to tell.'

'I have a few,' Dev said.

'We? So you have siblings?'

'I have one brother, Romesh, and…' He stopped talking and turned away, his voice tinged with something she couldn't read, all of a sudden.

'And?'

'Just one brother,' he finished. There it was, the same look he'd had when she'd caught him staring at his phone earlier. He sighed and turned back to the window, and before she could probe him any further, her own phone buzzed. Larissa, checking in again from Svalbard:

About to arrive at the hotel, and the cold is already too much. How is the heat of Kerala treating you? Also, jealous that it's hot and I hate you.

Ally couldn't help but snicker at the photo. Larry was bundled up in so many layers it was a wonder she could even move. She couldn't wait for a proper catch-up video call, as soon as possible.

'Everything OK?' Dev asked, arching an eyebrow at her sudden laughter.

'Fine,' Ally replied, deciding that she'd update her friend later. She huffed another laugh to herself, picturing Larry huddled up in an ice hut clutching a club. What did natives use to fend off polar bears over there? Surely they didn't shoot them, being nearly extinct and all. Dev was looking at her, head tilted at an angle.

'Sorry… I was just wondering if my friend has seen a polar bear yet,' she said, by way of explanation.

'Did she go to the zoo today?'

Ally baulked. Then she snorted a laugh that lasted longer than she'd planned it to. Composing herself, she explained the assignment her friend had taken for the same organisation in Svalbard and did not miss the slight look of alarm cross Dev's face. She had to wonder, was he alarmed at an unprepared GP from Somerset being stuck three feet from the North Pole, or at the thought of being stuck here, in Kerala, with her?

'So, how did you two end up on opposite sides of the world?'

'Long story short,' Ally began. 'Our clinic in Frome was closing down, and we both had to take assignments elsewhere. We challenged each other to have an adventure while we figure out what's next—and also to…' She stopped herself. No need to tell him she was supposed to have a fling. It had been her idea, even though she wasn't entirely sure she was over Matt enough to go there with anyone else. She'd done it more in solidarity with Larissa, who was still reeling over her break-up and really needed something or someone else to distract her.

'So, you want an adventure?' Dev's laughter filled the car, and she realised it was quite a lovely sound. She could feel the vibrations of it, almost like tiny tremors in the air, resonating through her body. It was a warm and comforting sensation that lingered after he stopped and made her want more. She'd felt guilty every time she'd laughed, since the accident. Like, how dared she find amusement and joy in anything after what happened to her boyfriend, and Nora's husband?

'How's that working out for you so far?'

'Too soon to tell,' Ally replied. But before they could delve any deeper, the car came to a stop. She followed his eyes to the palm-fringed field with its mountainous background and a circle of modest beige tents. Several other members of their team were climbing out of their respective Jeeps and starting to lift boxes and supplies. So this would be their home while they worked the vaccination drive. It wasn't too bad, she supposed. Outside on muddy ground, Ally couldn't help but steal another glance at Dev as, finally, he released his throat from his collar and insisted on wheeling her suitcase for her, along with his. What a gentleman.

Maybe the dashing Dr Chandran would play a role in fulfilling her and Larry's challenge, she thought, training her eyes on his pert backside. Then she caught herself. There was much more at stake here than just a fleeting romantic encounter. This placement was probably going to test her in so many ways and, as Nora had said, she needed to do something that wasn't wallowing in what could have been if...

No.

With a deep breath, Ally squared her shoulders and followed Dev into the camp.

CHAPTER TWO

THE HUM OF activity at the vaccination camp was like a beehive in full swing, and holy shiz, was it hot here. Ally felt as if she'd mostly been conducting her work from behind a sheen of highly unattractive sweat for the past few days, though she'd been administering vaccine after vaccine to the locals for an hour and a half today already.

Despite the important nature of the work, the chatter from people around the camp, and the muggy heat that clung to her skin, her attention kept veering towards Dev. Each time she glanced over, catching him in the midst of a task, she couldn't help but think back to the prospect of a fling. Something about him made her quite shy, and nervous. He was definitely the exact opposite of Matt, who'd always seemed so approachable, and affable and comforting. Matt, who, as a data analyst for one of Britain's top banks, would not have known what to do with himself in an outdoor space without computers. She'd always secretly wished Matt could talk more with her about her line of work, but she supposed it had always been nicer for him to come home and switch off from work talk completely.

Dev's tall, lean figure was bent attentively over a patient now, his thick dark hair falling forward as he worked. Even through the chaos, Ally couldn't help but note how the light caught the subtle contours of his muscles under his shirt. *Mmm.* Then, as though sensing his eyes on her from across the camp, he looked up, and caught her staring.

Oops.

'Next,' Ally called automatically as her current patient moved away, refusing to let her eyes wander back to Dev, where they would inevitably hover and embarrass her further. Mind you though, he did seem utterly focused on his work. She knew he was the kind of man she would trust if an emergency came up…as his previous role was as an emergency doctor. Here it was all hands on deck for the most part.

A little girl was talking to him now, showing him something she'd pulled from her pocket. Ally couldn't see what it was from here but the sight of him, so absorbed in his role and humouring the cute little girl, sent another unexpected and not so welcome flutter through her stomach. Every time it happened she had to wonder if it was him, or a burgeoning case of dysentery. You never knew in these remote locations, but so far it seemed to be just Dev causing it. She chastised herself silently.

Professionalism first, Ally.

With her water bottle running on empty for what felt like the tenth time already, Ally slipped away to the makeshift refreshment stand and filled it up, taking a giant swig and swiping at her brow. She could totally go for a nap after this round was done, the jet lag was still making her brain a little foggy, but she didn't think she'd get much sleep, even if she did lie down. The tightness of the camp meant privacy was a luxury. You could literally hear everything everyone did or said, thanks to the tents being packed so close together. Two more had appeared this morning for late arrivals, like mushrooms sprouting up after rain.

Her phone buzzed, and she yanked it from her skirt pocket under her white coat. Larissa!

Larissa had probably forgotten the four-hour time difference between them, but, to be fair, Ally had forgotten herself yesterday, calling her mid-afternoon. Svalbard was making her friend a bit glum, being so dark around the clock. Of course, she'd done her best to cheer her up thus far.

She answered the call, fanning herself with a napkin.

'Hey, you! Tell me everything. How's life in

the dark? How is your Thor lookalike?' she said, thinking back to another text where she'd told her about a hot Norwegian guy. It felt as if she'd known Larissa her whole life already, but really it had only been five or six years. They balanced each other out, like yin and yang. Plus Larry had been a rock when they'd lost Matt and Albie on that vacation from hell. She'd been so sure Matt was the one, that they'd grow old together discussing *The Great British Bake Off* over midweek biscuit binges. Bringing up two nutty kids in a three-bed semi with a fishpond in the garden. Planning the retirement cruise of their dreams.

What about the cruise? she'd wailed to Larissa in one particularly heavy bout of sobbing in the back room at the clinic.

I'll go with you, Larissa had promised. She would as well. Larry loved a bit of luxury. She also came over every week on cue for *Bake Off*, determined that it would be their tradition now Matt was gone.

Larry asked her if she'd spoken much to 'the hot guy from Canada you mentioned'. Ally sighed, and told her about last night's campfire dinner. They'd lined up for their meal of stewed meat and veggies, cooked in a giant pot in the makeshift kitchen area, and in the line, clutching their plates, they had had a brief conversation, where she'd asked him more about Toronto.

She'd learned that Dev's father had been some kind of big-deal doctor in Mumbai, who had been relocated to Canada, and now he was working on leveraging his expertise in minimally invasive spinal surgeries by co-founding a startup focused on developing an AI-powered surgical navigation system.

She'd asked about his siblings again, seeing as he'd stopped short in the car after mentioning that, but he'd made it seem as though it was a difficult topic for some reason. Then they'd been separated and sat at opposite ends of the table in the mess hall, which Dev had actually helped to construct yesterday. She relayed how she'd watched his muscles bulge as he'd lifted, hammered and sweated, till the mess hall had been surrounded by giant mosquito nets. It must have tired him out. He'd gone to bed even earlier than she had.

Before Larissa could ask more, a male voice resonated outside. Someone was calling her name, looking for her.

Ending the call, Ally stepped out of her tent, the world started whirring around her again, and someone called her name again. It was Aryan, the medical assistant who'd set up his station next to hers, but it was Dev's eye she caught from across the way as she brushed a loose strand of auburn hair from her face, tucking it behind her ear as she hurried her pace. A man was sitting in the seat at her stand, bent over slightly, and he looked up as she approached. He was middle-aged, she could see now from the creased lines of worry etching his forehead.

'Hello, I'm Nurse Spencer,' she said, her tone professional yet as soothing as she could muster. 'How can I help you today?'

'I've been feeling a bit dizzy lately, Nurse,' the man replied, his voice tinged with an accent that spoke of the local soil. 'And now there's this rash on my arm. Your colleague said you might take a look?'

'Let me take a look,' Ally said, gently examining the inflamed skin. The heat was unrelenting, and beads of sweat formed at her temples, but her focus remained sharp on the task at hand, even as she felt Dev's eyes on her again. Maybe, as the emergency doctor here, he felt he should be involved in any impromptu examinations?

'Excuse me, Dr Chandran?' she called out to him, raising an arm in the air. Dev was only a few steps away, overseeing another vaccination station. His last client was just rolling down her shirt sleeve. 'Could you have a quick look here?'

Dev glanced up yet again, his intense brown eyes momentarily locking with hers before he pushed back his chair and walked over. The sunlight danced off his charcoal-black hair as he moved towards her, creating a halo-like effect that was hard to ignore. There was a gracefulness to his stride too. Very different from how Matt had walked. Matt had kind of…well…plodded, to put it kindly. Her mum had always said he was a sixty-year-old in a thirty-year-old's body, but he had been quirky, and kind, and he'd loved her.

Dev's tall, lean form moved with ease through the crowded campsite, dodging children playing in the dirt and other medical staff scurrying from place to place. How could he bear his collar being buttoned up? she wondered momentarily. It was so hot. Casual, professional, and hot in more ways than one—this was Dev. He knelt beside the patient, observing the rash with his trained eye. 'Have you been feeling nauseous or experiencing any headaches?' he asked, his voice calm and measured.

'A bit of both, yes,' the man admitted.

'It looks like heat exhaustion to me, more than measles,' Dev concluded after a brief consultation. 'We should get him hydrated and into a cooler environment,' he said to her. 'Some oral rehydration salts would do the trick, along with a rest in the shade.'

'I was waiting a long time, and I rode here on my horse,' the man explained, using a tissue she provided to mop his bald head.

'Right.' Ally nodded, impressed with how

Dev had swiftly pinpointed the issue, and how he was now resting a hand sympathetically on the man's shoulder, encouraging him to stand with them. She could have treated him herself, really, but something about the way Dev had looked at her stepping out of her tent had made her want to close the gap between them. Together, they helped him towards a shaded area, one on each arm to assist him in his weariness, offering support with each step.

The man thanked them profusely, his gratitude for their joint efforts evident, despite the discomfort etched on his face, and the language barrier. Dev was translating everything, though body language spoke volumes in medical situations. Ally fetched the necessary supplies and handed them to their patient with instructions.

'Take care and make sure to drink plenty of fluids,' Ally told him, leaving him in her assistant Aryan's care, before catching Dev on the way back to his stand.

'Thank you for your valuable input,' she fibbed, her heart skipping briefly at the approval in his eyes.

'It wasn't the toughest case I've had to tend to,' he said, and his mouth flipped up at one corner, as if he was suppressing an amused smirk.

'Well…it's always good to get a second opinion,' she retorted, fanning out her white coat over her shirt. His eyes travelled to her cleavage for half a second, and it made the blood zip about her body like a flock of mosquitoes. A new feeling completely, since Matt's death, and one she wasn't entirely sure what to do with: was this part of her she'd assumed to be dead still struggling for attention deep down somewhere? What to do with it? A fling…perhaps…just to see if her libido was still as alive as it was starting to seem?

For the next couple of hours, she watched Dev interact with his patients from across the camp, which included a couple of injuries, as well as administering the vaccines. Ally couldn't help but notice the tenderness in his touch as he saw to one of the young girls who'd been playing around the camp, the kid of a local volunteer. His large hands were careful and precise on her scraped knee, cleaning the wound with an expertise and a kindness that were fascinating and endearing to watch, even to her, an experienced nurse. There was something about the way he held the girl's gaze as she sniffled, reassuring her without words, that made Ally's chest tighten. As if he was lost somewhere in his head, at the same time as seeming entirely present. Who *was* Dev Chandran?

She had to get him alone and ask him more about himself. Maybe he would be fling material, but she'd have to crack him open a bit first.

He seemed to hold a well of secrets beneath that cool, preppy and composed exterior. That much was evident by the way he'd fobbed her off when she'd asked about his siblings again yesterday. It made her wonder if he was involved in some kind of argument with a family member. People didn't work endless stints in random places with the NHF unless they were running away from something back home. She should know, she thought guiltily, thinking of Nora living out the same routine as usual, without her. Ally wasn't running exactly, but she had thought it might be nice to see a place Matt had wanted to see, and, at the same time, get away from all the stuff that still reminded her of him for a while. It wasn't as if she'd be gone for long…she would never. Nora needed her.

'How do you manage to make everyone feel so at ease when it's a thousand degrees out here?' she asked him later, when she met him at the water dispenser. The team were like elephants congregating around a spring, the amount of water they seemed to drink out here.

'You just get used to it,' Dev said, brushing off the compliment as he cleaned his hands with sanitiser. 'But I could say the same about you.'

'Oh, really,' Ally allowed, feeling her lips curving upwards as her mind raced with the fact that he'd clearly been watching her at work, too. 'But I still think you have a magic touch.'

Oh, God, was she flirting now?

She was terrible at it and should most definitely stop.

'Magic, huh?' Dev chuckled softly, a slight sparkle lighting his eyes again as she fanned her coat, almost inviting him to check out her cleavage again.

Ally, you are a traitor to yourself!

He refrained, anyway. Instead, he cleared his throat and looked at her face from under thick black eyelashes that should really be illegal on men due to the desperate unfairness of it. 'I'll have to remember that one.'

'Please do,' Ally replied as her heart continued to rev up to top gear. OK, yes, she was flirting, apparently. She could almost imagine Larry egging her on. So why was she more nervous than excited, all of a sudden, feeling his curiosity pique around her and his eyes rove her breasts through her sweaty clothes? He held her gaze, amusement lighting his eyes, and she struggled to pinpoint why she found the prospect of being romantically involved with anyone for *any* amount of time so disconcerting. Matt was gone. He'd been gone for two years.

A flashback struck her. Herself and her devastated sister, collapsed in the driveway of their

rented villa in Palermo in front of the Sicilian po-
licemen. Oliver sobbing, both of them taking it
in turns to comfort him, despite breaking apart
themselves. Albie and Matt had been taken from
them so suddenly, in the most tragic of ways. A
dog walker had found their bloated bodies on a
nearby beach and they'd heard the helicopters
before the news. The broken boat had sunk half
a mile from the shore. Just when they'd assumed
their lives couldn't have been going better. You
just never really got over something like that.

With a steadying breath, Ally turned to the
supply tent. She needed more needles and gauze
already…and air. A volunteer helped her locate
what she needed, and she balanced a box on top
of another. Why make two trips across camp
when she could make one? She was just making
her way back across the grass, three feet from the
tent, when a sudden movement caught her eye
over the top of the boxes. Smooth, sleek-furred,
and undeniably feline, the creature padded quietly into her path, and promptly came to a stop
in front of her.

Leopard.

Ally's heart thudded against her ribcage, the
top box slipping from her limp fingers as she
stifled a scream.

She took a shaky step backwards, her eyes
locked on the agile, prowling cat in front of her.

She had seen leopards on TV before, but never in person. And certainly not this close. She could make out every spot, every stroke of its fur. Its eyes were narrowed towards her, as if it were saying, *How dare this human cross my path?*

'Ally, freeze!' Dev's voice cut through the bustling noise of the campsite, sharp as a scalpel. 'It won't hurt you if you don't move. Keep eye contact, that's imperative.'

Ally could feel the sweat trickling down her back as she tried to stay completely still. *Oh, God...is this how I die?*

Time seemed to twist and stretch as every atom of her filled with dread. Her skin prickled with beads of sweat. Every frantic beat of her heart seemed to echo the tremor in her limbs as, from the corner of her eye, she saw Dev creep up slowly behind the cat, holding a long, pointed object. Was he serious? She saw him motion to the wide-eyed onlookers, but what he was telling them, she couldn't tell.

'Whatever you do, don't move an inch,' he instructed again, his tone a strange mixture of calm and urgency that somehow rooted her to the spot even more, even as her gaze stayed locked on the leopard's cold, unblinking eyes. The box she was still holding seemed to weigh a thousand tonnes. Every instinct screamed at her to run, but Ally knew the leopard's strike would be swifter than any movement she dared make. What was it even doing here? Was this normal?

The camp had gone eerily silent, all activity paused as eyes turned towards the human-versus-leopard stand-off. Dev was still creeping closer, and closer. He was holding a long wooden tent peg, she realised. He must have yanked it out of one of the tents. Suddenly, the leopard did a turn, making to face Dev and the crowd instead of her. She sucked in a breath and prepared for the worst as Dev threw his arms in the air, signalling for the onlookers. Just then, everyone in the camp started yelling at the top of their lungs. Some were throwing sticks in the stunned creature's direction.

'Get out of here,' Dev commanded it, waving the tent peg with intent. She could finally move and darted sideways as a shower of sticks landed around the creature. Then, miraculously, the huge cat finally seemed to think better about being here. It slunk away again into the underbrush, disappearing as quickly as it had appeared.

Ally's knees wobbled. She dropped the remaining box and stumbled backwards, only to be steadied by Dev's firm grip on her arm. The campsite seemed to exhale in collective relief, the sound rustling through the trees like a released breath. *What the heck just happened?*

'Are you OK?' Dev peered into her face. Those

intense brown eyes shimmered with genuine concern and she forced herself to calm down, even though her heart was still a drum.

'Y-yes,' she stammered, trying to regain her composure. 'Thanks to you.'

'Quick thinking,' a volunteer acknowledged, and in seconds Dev was receiving pats on the back from everyone who passed. He was only looking at her, however.

'I owe you my life. You just faced a leopard with a tent peg,' Ally said incredulously, her voice a whisper as the magnitude of what could have happened began to sink in. A look of strange determination crossed his face, mixed with something else she couldn't put her finger on.

'Let's get you sitting down for a moment,' he suggested, guiding her to a nearby chair. As she sat, the cool touch of his hand stayed on her shoulder, grounding her. Meeting his gaze, she tried to thank him, but then she saw a depth of caring on his face that went beyond the call of duty. It made her heart start to flutter all over again in a way that had nothing to do with fear. 'We lost a newborn baby to a leopard a few months ago in Nepal,' he told her.

'Oh, no, that's terrible. What happened?'

'Dragged it right out of the cradle. Lucky we didn't lose you, too,' he said, 'or anyone else here.'

Ally didn't miss how his hand remained on her shoulder and his eyes lingered on hers for a moment longer than he seemed to feel comfortable with, before he excused himself and walked back to his stand. He did cast a look back at her as he took his seat again, and as the adrenaline slowed its course through her body, she knew she probably owed Dev more than a fling, if she ever got up the courage to initiate anything. She might just owe him her life!

CHAPTER THREE

DEV STOOD BY the Jeep next to Ally as the school-yard slowly filled with the children, pouring out of the classrooms to gape at the newcomers, their uniforms patched but clean. The school building where they were due to run today's vaccination drive was modest, as schools in most small towns out here in Kerala tended to be, painted a once-vibrant yellow that he knew would have been significantly dulled by the sun and time. In Toronto, this amount of chipped paint would probably be considered unsafe.

For a brief moment he thought of his nephew in Toronto: Romesh's son, Nikki. When was the last time he'd seen Nikki? The last time he'd gone home for that horrific family gathering three years ago, he thought guiltily.

Ally had a smile across her face as she started greeting them, humouring their curiosity.

'Looks like we're the main event here,' she quipped, her pale blue eyes twinkling with humour despite the early hour. He enjoyed how she seemed to find the humour in everything, even though it set him on edge. People who did that tended to be hiding something underneath, something they didn't want to face, or know *how* to face. He should know.

'Seems so,' he agreed, his attention briefly snagging on her long, wavy auburn hair as it caught the golden glow of the morning sun. She was unquestionably pretty, with her milky white skin, despite the sun's capacity to burn its way across her slanted cheekbones. He'd caught himself watching her far too much all week, but it was lucky he'd been watching her when that leopard had crept up the other day. Otherwise…who knew?

They hadn't really talked much since. He'd been wanting to, but he knew she would ask him questions about his life, as she'd started to that first night in the line for dinner in their makeshift mess hall, and he wasn't about to get too personal, too soon. Especially not with someone as attractive as Ally.

The last time he'd got too personal with a co-worker on one of these assignments, it had ended with her fleeing the programme altogether, claiming she couldn't work with someone she was in love with, especially someone who didn't appear to love her back. Cassinda, the Brazilian-American, had done her best to dirty his reputation before and after leaving, even if no one had really given it much credit, thankfully, but he'd sworn not to get involved with a co-worker ever again. The last thing he needed was more guilt on top of the load he was always carrying. He was here to get away from that. Not that he ever escaped it, really. It just followed him.

A flicker of Roisin's smiling face crossed his mind for just a second. He should have gone home at Christmas, gone to her grave with the rest of his family, but he still couldn't bear it, knowing it was his fault his sister was dead; knowing they all knew it was his fault, even though they never said it.

The kids were upon them now, chattering in Malayalam, their smiles wide and welcoming as ever. He always enjoyed his stints in Kerala, but this one was proving more interesting already, purely because of this white woman with her funny English accent and high-pitched, infectious laugh. Ally crouched to their level effortlessly in her flowing blue skirt, responding with high fives. He had noticed this all week, how the kids around the campsite all responded to her warmth like flowers to the sun, basking in her attentiveness.

'Ally's got a knack with them, doesn't she?' Rani, their community outreach coordinator, noted from behind him, watching the scene unfold.

'Definitely,' Dev murmured, more to himself than to Rani. It was one thing to be good at your job, quite another to radiate care as naturally as breathing. Ally did both, without seeming to realise how rare that combination was. He had seen a lot throughout his time with NHF, a lot of people from a lot of places, and while he didn't really know why she was here, aside from her clinic back home closing down and forcing her out of a job, he had a feeling she wasn't the type to stay away from home for long. Just by looking at her, he could tell she probably had kids of her own, or at least in her family, that she was used to spending time with.

As for him, he'd been doing everything in his power *not* to go home and face his family. He thought a little guiltily back to his mother's email, still unanswered in his inbox. She'd asked what his plans were for Valentine's Day, aka Roisin's birthday. He would let her down gently, he decided, tell them he had a new assignment, even if he didn't. The annual get-together in honour of the love they'd had, and still had, for his little sister always got the what-ifs torturing him all over again. What if he hadn't let her ride with him in the passenger seat? What if he'd taken the usual route home instead of a shortcut?

He would let Mom down gently soon, he decided. Maybe when they stopped at the next place, when the Internet was better. *Always some excuse,* he thought as the guilt kicked in again.

The vaccination drive thankfully all went to plan in the shade of the trees outside the school. Dev found himself observing Ally when she wasn't looking. Her wide gestures and ebullient mannerisms made it hard not to. Twin boys, no older than six, seemed particularly taken with her ahead of their vaccines. They wore identical shorts and shirts, which meant they were impossible to tell apart. The fabric of their clothes was faded like the school building, washed and hung to dry in the sun too many times, but her jokes were making them giggle and nudge each other conspiratorially. He finished with his last patient, and his feet seemed to find their own way over to her somehow.

'OK, you two,' Ally was saying when he reached her side. 'Ready to be super brave for me?'

They nodded vigorously, apparently unaffected by any fear of needles.

'Braver than Superman?' Dev chimed in, hoping to share in the moment. Ally caught his eye and gave him a sideways smile from behind her hair, and he felt something tighten in his chest as he pulled at his collar in the heat.

'Braver than Spiderman!' one of the twins declared, puffing out his chest.

'I'm braver than both of them!' the other added,

not to be outdone. Clearly they had been learning English at this school already, or they watched a lot of TV.

Ally laughed, ruffling their hair affectionately before instructing them to stay still, and administering the vaccines with a steady hand. The twins didn't flinch. In fact, their gazes were locked on Ally as if she'd woven a spell around them.

'See? You are superheroes. You didn't even feel it,' she praised, handing each of them a sticker.

'Thanks, Ally *chechi*!' they chorused. Dev felt his eyebrows rise. They were using the Malayalam term for older sister. It was rare people took to the volunteers as fast as this. The last time he'd been so impressed by someone's effortlessly easy-going nature was during the stint he'd done in Nepal, with Cassinda. He'd been so drawn to her and missing that vital flesh-to-flesh connection that resisting her powers of seduction late one night had been impossible. How was he to know she'd promptly fall in love with him and expect him to stop working for the NHF at the end of their fling, to go with her back to America, start a family?

As if he were ever going to stop moving. He'd thrown himself into it for the last seven years, thinking that by helping others in need, maybe he could somehow atone for the loss he'd caused his family. It hadn't worked yet. It would never work, and why would it? But each time he moved, he had a new chance to try…and another excuse not to go home and face the pain he'd caused his parents and Romesh.

That fling with Cassinda was definitely the *last* one he'd have on the job, though. These hook-ups never got him anywhere, and never made him feel anything other than guilt when they ended.

His thoughts flew from his head when he saw Ally. 'Good work, Nurse,' he said when she stood up, her face flushed with the joy of doing what she obviously loved.

'Thanks, Dev.' She brushed off her hands, unaware of the admiration she'd garnered. Least of all from him. She had a stunning body, he thought, wondering if that weird-sounding place she lived—Frome—had a good yoga studio, or whether she just got arms that toned from lifting other kinds of weights, like boxes and…babies?

Ally paused, locking eyes with him for a brief second, as if she might've caught a glimpse of his thoughts. 'What does *chechi* mean?' she asked.

He told her and she nodded, eyebrows hitched. 'I like to think I've been a good sister.' She paused. 'But then I think, if I *was* a good sister, would I really be all the way out here away from Nora?'

He frowned at her, her words going around in his head. He almost asked what she meant exactly but, by the look on her face, it seemed like one of those things that was best left unaddressed by a relative stranger such as himself. She almost looked sad. 'You have a sister?'

'Nora. We're close, but it doesn't exactly make me sibling of the year.'

'Well, I'm not exactly a great brother myself,' he heard himself say, thinking of Romesh, and she offered him a half-smile with questions in her own eyes. Then the moment passed, and Ally was swept away, leaving Dev with the echo of a brief connection he wasn't sure was safe to explore.

The vaccination drive was a whirlwind of activity again in the afternoon. The children wanted to show them everything.

'*Chechi, chechi*, come see!' the twins exclaimed. They'd been hovering around Ally all day and now she was allowing herself to be led across the schoolyard, her face reflecting wonder and delight every time she was shown something else: a ball, a toy, a drawing, and now...

'Look, the hummingbirds!' one of the twins pointed out, his small hand gesturing towards the flurry of wings suspended near a patch of wildflowers.

Dev rose from his seat. His nephew, Nikki, had loved the hummingbirds at the sanctuary in Toronto, last time he was home. Crossing the dusty forecourt, then the grass, he positioned himself just close enough to observe without in-truding. The hummingbirds were a spectacle as they usually were, even more so in their natural habitat, he thought, all iridescent feathers glinting in the sunlight as they hovered and dipped with an elegance that defied the rapid beat of their wings. Ally's attention was fully on the birds as she knelt beside the boys, who were armed with paintbrushes and palettes of watercolours. So this was art class.

'You can paint them too, Ally *chechi*,' one boy said expectantly.

'Let's see about that—art was never my strongest subject,' she replied, her voice playful. Dev watched as she dipped a brush into a pool of cobalt blue and the twins leaned in, their eyes wide with amazement as colours bloomed onto the paper in the form of another hummingbird. She'd lied, she was actually a pretty good artist. And right now he kind of wanted to paint her too. Her hair was the colour of leaves in the fall; a special kind of red you found only in Canada. He sniffed, making her turn her head to him.

'Isn't it amazing how they just hang in the air?' she mused.

'Like magic,' one of the twins whispered.

'Exactly like magic,' she agreed, turning back to the boy, but not before Dev felt as if she'd seen something in his gaze that he wasn't entirely comfortable showing her. Yes, he would love to spend more time with Ally away from the camp and their work, but that kind of thinking wasn't going to do him any favours.

She carried on painting, and her laughter mingled with that of the twin boys, an infectious sound that brightened the entire schoolyard and brought more and more of the children over, all with paintbrushes of their own. He wondered what Nikki was doing now, as he often did. Did he ever think about his uncle all the way out here, or had he forgotten him by now?

'Dev, you're awfully quiet over there,' Ally called out. 'Everything OK?'

'Just thinking about logistics for tomorrow,' he lied smoothly.

'Right,' Ally said, not looking entirely convinced but letting it slide. She turned back to the twins, guiding their small hands as they attempted to mimic the iridescence of the hummingbirds on paper. But he didn't miss the way she kept turning back to him, looking at him when she didn't think he would notice.

Later that evening, as the flames from the campfire crackled, Dev found himself sitting beside Ally on a fallen log, the rest of their team scattered around.

'Can I ask you something?' Ally's voice was soft but carried a thread of determination. It made Dev brace himself internally.

'Go ahead,' he responded, watching as the flames consumed the wood with a fervour.

'Earlier today…with the boys, you seemed… distant. More than just tired. Is everything all right?'

Her pale blue eyes searched his face and Dev took a deep breath, feeling the warmth from the fire battling the chill that had nothing to do with the night air. 'It's just—seeing those twins today reminded me of my nephew, Nikki.' His admission hung between them like the smoke from the campfire, curling upwards and dissipating into the night sky. 'He looks just like my brother.'

'How old is he?' Ally prodded gently, probably sensing quite correctly that there was more he wasn't saying.

'He'll be nine soon. I haven't seen him in a long time. I don't go back to Canada often.' As the words exited his mouth he could almost hear them echoing the distance he felt.

'Why not?'

'Busy, I guess,' he said quickly. Then he felt bad for the lie. 'Well, maybe that's an excuse. Home is…not exactly my favourite place to be.'

Ally reached out, placing a hand on his arm,

and her simple gesture felt laden with the kind of empathy that had drawn him to her before, when his feet had led him to her side of their own accord. 'I'm sorry to hear that, Dev,' she said.

He chewed his lip as they watched their co-workers chatting amongst themselves, swigging tea from tin cups. Ally was looking at him again. He could tell she wanted to ask why home was not his favourite place, and why he didn't go very often, but she didn't.

'I never thanked you properly for saving my life,' she told him.

'Yeah, you did,' he replied. 'But there's no need to thank me, really.' He poked a stick at the glowing embers, sending a shower of sparks up into the night. The firelight flickered across her face as she leaned forward. 'Most of the wildlife is more afraid of us than we are of them. We just have to keep our wits about us in the more remote locations.'

'Got it,' she said, smirking. 'As long as I don't see any snakes.'

'You will,' he assured her, and she winced. 'Snakes are great. I had a snake once in Toronto. A ball python called Monty.'

'You actually owned a snake?' She sounded horrified, and he bit back a smile at the look on her face. Mentioning Monty—a gift from his brother to keep him company during late study nights at med school—did tend to conjure images of serpents slithering through grass with evil intent.

'He was one of the gentlest creatures you could ever meet,' Dev continued.

'I never took you for a snake enthusiast,' Ally said, brushing her auburn hair back.

Dev shrugged. 'I've always been fascinated by them.'

'I suppose some animals rely on humans seeing beyond what scares them.'

'And sometimes humans need the same thing,' he found himself saying.

Ally nodded quietly. 'Speaking of animals, Nora—my sister—she has this cat,' she began, her voice softening. 'He's been such a comfort to her, especially…after Albie.'

'Albie?' Dev felt his brows furrow slightly.

'Her husband, my brother-in-law. We lost him two years ago,' Ally said, the words falling heavily between them. 'I've been living with her since then, helping with my eight-year-old nephew. It's been…a lot.' She drew in a sharp breath and hugged her knees.

'Ally, that's… I'm sorry to hear that,' he replied after a pause. 'How did he die, if you don't mind me asking?'

'He drowned.'

Oh. God.

Suddenly, the happy front she seemed to show the world became a lot more nuanced and it deepened his respect for her on the spot. But she shrugged off the weight of the memory quickly, as if she was regretting telling him already. 'We all carry something with us, don't we?' she said, forcing a small smile. 'Baggage.' The second she said it, she looked as if she wanted to kick herself.

'True,' he agreed, and for a second he almost told her about the accident that killed Roisin while he was beside her in the driver's seat, without so much as a scratch on him, but he kept his words to himself. The fewer people knew about that the better. At least out here he could simply be himself. People saw him just as Dev, instead of an extension of the tragedy, which was how he viewed himself most of the time.

'Speaking of baggage, that was some suitcase you arrived here with.' He nudged her and she chuckled, and they fell into silence, and the crackling of the fire punctuated his thoughts like hot rods, poking into his wounds. How could he not think about *Ally's* struggles now? She'd lost a family member, whereas he had distanced himself from his on purpose when they were all he had. As if he needed anything else to feel guilty about!

Quietly he excused himself and made his way to his tent, but he could feel Ally's eyes on his back the whole way there.

CHAPTER FOUR

ALLY STIFLED A yawn as the Jeep trundled along the rugged path, weaving through the lush landscape on the way back from the school to the campsite. Her gaze wandered outside the window, taking in the blur of greenery and wildflowers that lined the roadside. A rustic sign loomed ahead, its arrow pointing towards the Edakkal Caves.

'Look at that,' Dev said from behind the wheel. His voice yanked her attention back inside the vehicle instantly.

'Edakkal Caves,' Ally echoed, leaning forward to get a better view of the sign. 'I've noticed it before, but I've got no idea what's there, do you?'

'I don't know, caves, I guess,' he said with a shrug, and she smirked as his dark eyes briefly met hers before refocusing on the road. There was an ease about him at times, when he wasn't doing that dark, brooding thing, that Ally admired, a calmness that seemed to run as deep as his Indian roots. Still, he made her so hot. Dev was the perfect fling material. But aside from their few brief conversations, which had only left her wondering more about him, she still knew barely anything about the man.

She couldn't help but think back to when they'd sat around the campfire, and what he'd told her about not going home much. He'd said that home wasn't somewhere he enjoyed particularly. He'd seemed almost sad about it, as if he *couldn't* go home, for some reason. So mysterious.

Her own words echoed in her mind too. She'd told him how Albie died, and the consequent shadow it had cast over her family, but she hadn't been able to tell him Matt had died too, on the same day, in the same horrific accident.

If she'd started down that path, she would've had to offer details, but she was out here to be someone people could respect and have a fun time with, as well as rely on to get the job done. She was not here to invite glances and whispers over having a dead brother-in-law *and* a dead boyfriend. One of the trash mags had contacted her weeks after the accident, fishing for the 'shocking family story', offering four hundred quid. She'd told them to shove it. Then they'd had the audacity to contact Nora instead, who had also told them to shove it.

But she'd been moved by the sympathetic tilt of Dev's head, and how his brown eyes had held a universe of unspoken understanding. They'd barely known each other a fortnight but she'd dwelled on it afterwards in a call to Larissa. Larissa had of course told her to jump on him. She was meant to be having a fling, not looking for emotional connections! Not that *she* wasn't still holding herself back from pouncing on her Svalbard man, Thor, for one reason or another. Larissa said they'd been talking, and that she was kind of obsessed with his dog, called Midnight, but she'd also called Ally to ask how to tell him that she wanted to sleep with him! Maybe they were both a bit worried about developing feelings for someone?

'Can I ask you something?' Ally ventured, her fingers nervously twisting a lock of her hair. She was thinking she should ask Dev the same thing, but she wasn't as bold as she was pretending to be, obviously.

'Of course,' Dev replied, casting a quick glance in her direction.

'Do you think…?' She paused, unsure how to frame her thoughts without *sounding* insecure. 'Last night, when I told you about my brother-in-law, do you think it might seem like I'm running away from all my responsibilities back home? It only happened two years ago. Nora says she's OK but she's not. I know she's not.'

Dev considered her question, his eyes fixed on

the winding road. For a moment, the only sound was the Jeep's tyres crunching over gravel and the distant call of a bird.

'Ally,' he said with gentle sincerity, 'it's not for me to judge why anyone takes a job this far from home.'

His words carried a hint of his own issues. He'd got up so fast last night, and exited their conversation before it had really got going. Ally had felt the intrigue building all night after that, her heart skipping a beat at the prospect of peeling back the layers of Dev, fixing her mouth to his on the pillow in his tent between his pouring out his deepest fears. Gosh, it was too hot and, thanks to Larissa, she was getting ahead of herself. *Way* ahead.

'Thanks,' she murmured, fanning out her top. He shot her a sideways glance and his mouth twitched in that way it did when he found her amusing.

'Sounds like it's been a heavy couple of years,' he said. 'Maybe you deserve some fun.'

Ally felt her next words catch in her throat. Had he read her mind, or had he been thinking about a little fling, too? The conversation around the campfire, while brief, had been unexpectedly intimate and here, in the daylight, this playful dance of attraction and intrigue going on between them was almost too obvious to deny. No wonder he was asking her.

'Shall we check out these caves, then?' he said, already signalling to turn off the main road.

Oh. OK. So that was what he meant by fun. He was a nerd at heart. Just as Matt had been. Only he was way better at the whole 'being intense and broody' thing, she thought. His eyes had been on her all day today, just like yesterday, and the day before. He hadn't been able to stop himself watching her, and she hadn't been able to stop herself staring at him either, or standing next to him every opportunity, under every guise: fetching water, fetching supplies, assisting an emergency he'd encountered with a young volunteer and an infected leg injury. But they were colleagues. They were professionals with an entire team around them. While it was intriguing to feel these things again, was it really a good idea to entertain them? She was already imagining pressing him against a rocky cave wall and devouring him.

Say no, stay professional, Ally! No way should you enter a cave with this man.

'Let's do it,' she said, a smile creeping onto her lips. What was one little adventure? Besides, Larry would kill her if she kept procrastinating over her mission—the whole fling thing had been *her* idea!

The Jeep veered off the main path, crunching over foliage as Dev steered towards the Edakkal Caves. Whatever they held was a mystery—how exciting. The lush Kerala landscape rolled by like an emerald sea. She loved how the towering trees brushed against the sky, their leaves whispering the secrets of their ancient history in a language they would never understand, maybe hiding Dev's favourite pets—snakes. Ugh. But interesting. Not like the boring shrubbery and weeds back home. The air here was thick with the scent of damp earth and wildflowers and, with Dev beside her, she couldn't deny the excitement bubbling inside her already.

'So, you said you don't go home a lot,' she said, breaking the silence. Well, she couldn't help that he intrigued her. 'Why is that? Is Toronto just too boring now?' She could sense it was more than that, but she was trying to be polite.

'I don't know,' he said, wriggling his nose. 'Maybe *I'm* the one who's running away from my responsibilities.' There was a hint of self-reflection in his voice that made Ally turn to study his profile.

'What do you mean?' she ventured, thinking maybe it had something to do with his brother, Romesh. 'If you don't mind me saying, you seem a little…off…whenever you mention your brother. Is it because of him?'

Damn it, was that too many questions? She fanned her shirt again. Why could she never read a room and shut up?

'Kind of,' he said with a non-committal shrug. She looked at him apologetically, but the corner of his mouth twitched up and she could tell he didn't mind her questions really. It didn't mean he was going to answer any of them. 'It's complicated. Here we are, let's see what these caves are all about!'

Dev parked the Jeep in a clearing surrounded by a cluster of trees and they got out, the sounds of the forest enveloping them instantly. They followed a narrow path that snaked its way through the underbrush and led to the entrance of the caves. Ally couldn't help her own mouth gaping open at the sheer size of the gaping mouth of the cave before them, the way the rocky walls seemed to swallow the light.

'Whoa,' she breathed, her voice echoing into the cavernous space ahead and bouncing back around her ears. Another bird took flight somewhere close by.

'Right?' Dev agreed, his eyes lighting up with the same sense of wonder that Ally felt.

'There won't be any bats, will there?' she said, suddenly wary.

'I thought you'd love a superhero's lair,' he teased, and she rolled her eyes, secretly pleased he remembered what she'd been laughing about with those adorable twin boys. They entered the dark, dank space side by side, and the coolness of the cave wrapped around them like a secret cloak. The walls were rough to the touch, moist with condensation, and the farther they ventured in, the more the outside world seemed to fall away.

Ally could hear the measured cadence of her own breaths and the soft scuff of their shoes against the stone floor. The light faded the deeper they went, his silhouette a reassuring contrast against the dimly lit passages. Every so often, their arms brushed, and a jolt of electricity passed between them and made her skin buzz.

'Careful here,' he murmured as they approached a narrower section of the cave. His hand found the small of her back, guiding her gently. The touch was fleeting but intimate and Ally's pulse raced in response.

'I'm always careful,' she managed, her voice sounding small in the vastness of the enclosed space. The tension between them was a living thing that danced in the slivers of light that could still reach this secluded corner of…wherever they were! She wasn't quite sure how to navigate this cave, let alone this attraction. Wait till she told Larissa about this.

'Whoa, check it out!' She stepped forward, her eyes tracing the outlines of figures etched into the rock face. Dev was beside her in a heartbeat, following her pointed finger. The ancient petro-glyphs were stretched across the walls like a sto-ryboard of a time that no one alive now would ever know. In the dim light, the images seemed to move, as if the carvings and stories they told were coming to life before her.

'My nephew, Oliver, would lose his mind over this,' she said in awe, picturing the boy's face. She felt a pang of missing him, followed by the guilt over leaving him and Nora, but she snuffed it out. Nora had wanted her to come here, she'd encouraged it. Ally wasn't avoiding responsibil-ities. Or was she? Ugh, this was not the time to think about it.

'Look at this one,' Dev said softly, his voice bouncing off the stone and wrapping around her. He pointed to a cluster of shapes that Ally hadn't noticed, his fingers mere inches from the carv-ings.

'An animal of some sort?' she said, leaning closer to inspect the image. Her shoulder brushed against his arm, sending a subtle thrill through her.

'Maybe a hunting scene,' he proposed, his gaze following the lines and curves with an academic interest that was undercut by the wonder in his tone. It made her smile. He was such a nerd. 'See how the figures seem to be chasing it?'

Ally nodded. The excitement in his voice was infectious, the way his curiosity shone through drawing her in like an expeditioner discovering new frontiers or something. She moved to another section of the wall, her hand hovering over a series of intricate designs, careful not to touch. 'And these? Rituals, maybe?'

'Could be,' he agreed, peering at the petroglyphs. His closeness enveloped her, and for a moment she forgot about the drawings, acutely aware of Dev's proximity, the sound of his breath, and the weird but tangible mutual attraction in what would, with anyone else, be a horribly claustrophobic space. She hated small spaces. One time she'd got stuck in a changing room and had been so freaked out she'd called 999. She told this to Dev, and he laughed. He had such a nice laugh.

They walked on together, stopping at various markings that caught their eye. The cave air was cool, a stark contrast to the humidity outside, and it felt as though they were in another world.

'Amazing to think that, centuries ago, people stood right where we are now,' she said in awe, breaking a new, more comfortable silence.

'And that they left their stories behind for us to find,' Dev added, his tone reflective. 'It makes you wonder about the legacies we'll leave. If anyone will remember us at all.'

The weight of his words settled on Ally's shoulders like lead. 'I think you're a pretty memorable person,' she heard herself say. He said nothing, but when he turned to look at her, his brown eyes seemed even more intense in the shadowy light. It made her keep talking. 'And your legacy is that you help people. Your work—our work—it's important. Those months after Matt and Albie died, I threw myself into it. I suppose I felt a bit like, if I could take away someone else's pain, then maybe some of mine might disappear along with it. I suppose maybe I was right...well, I'm getting there at least.'

Dev had stopped looking at the wall. His eyes were on her now, with a frown that she realised was the result of her slip-up.

'Matt *and* Albie?' he said.

She swallowed, suddenly hot. She hadn't told him about Matt.

'Matt was my boyfriend,' she admitted, her voice suddenly small. There was no air in here. Dev said nothing, he just pressed a hand over hers, stepped closer. She couldn't quite breathe right all of a sudden, his eyes were just too sympathetic, too close, yet she couldn't look away.

'He died when Albie did, on the boat, they went fishing...' She trailed off, swallowing back the lump that wasn't so much the result of saying it out loud but the way he was looking at her. 'Sorry, I can't...'

'It's OK,' was all he said, covering her whole hand with one of his. Her fingers felt safe, consumed by his warm palm, and despite her confession a zing shot through her stomach, making her heart feel as though he'd plugged her directly into some invisible caveman socket. 'Ally, I'm so sorry.'

'Thank you,' she said, forcing herself to stand taller, but not moving her hand. 'Like I said, it was two years ago.'

'That's like...still fresh,' he said, still looking at her as if he expected her to crumble into pieces and float away. She dropped his hand. Her neck and her palms were sweatier than before. He looked as if he was going to say something, but he didn't and she was glad. She probably couldn't have found the words or the breath to reply, but as they continued deeper into the cave, Ally's mind churned. He must have questions for her, just as she did for him.

'Thank you for this,' she said finally. 'For suggesting we come here. It's amazing.'

Dev nodded, but the jovial mood was pretty dead by now. 'I'm glad you wanted to check it out. It's not every day you get to walk through history with someone who appreciates it as much as you do.'

The compliment landed softly in Ally's chest, and the zing she'd felt before settled into a mild buzz that seemed to lift her without threatening to short-circuit her heart. She hadn't intended to tell him about Matt back there, but the words had tumbled out anyway. Maybe it was a good thing? She hadn't exactly shared any of this with anyone except her sister and Larry, but the combination of being so far away and spreading the info out, dispersing it in different places, felt a little less like releasing something vital to her existence into the wild, and more like the start of setting herself free.

At the next petroglyph Dev turned to her, his expression unreadable in the shifting shadows. 'I really am sorry about your brother-in-law, Ally, and your boyfriend. You don't have to talk about it. But I wouldn't blame you at all if you were running away. Stuff like that is hard to handle. I mean, it's hard to know how.' His jaw shifted from side to side for a moment. He was speaking from experience, she could tell.

'So what about you? There's a story there, isn't there?' she prodded gently.

Dev shifted, directing her onwards, away from the walls and onto the path ahead. 'I don't usually talk about my life outside work,' he said, his tone guarded.

'OK,' Ally said, tilting her head as she followed

him. For a while, he walked in silence, stroking his big manly fingers softly over the walls as if the rocks could read him their history like brail. But his stance spoke volumes, as if he was weighing the cost of his secrecy against the trust she could feel building between them, slowly. Slowly, but irrefutably. Which was strange, considering…well…everything. His shoulders came up around his ears for a moment and he flinched before swiping a hand across his jaw, all with his back to her.

'I lost my sister, seven years ago,' he relented with a sigh, stopping in his tracks. 'In Toronto. I was the one driving. Roisin was in the passenger seat. The car hit her side, head-on. She died instantly.'

His sentences entered her ears like a bullet, shattering into separate words that splintered into even tinier fragments, all of which struck her heart like an explosion. For a moment, she was speechless. Her hand came up over her mouth, and the other reached for him, grappling a void for a second before she somehow found his hand.

'Oh, Dev.'

'I'm the reason we lost her.'

She sucked another breath in, willing the right words to form. They wouldn't. All she could feel was his pain, as if he were holding up a mirror at the top of a well, forcing her own emotions back to the surface in a giant bucket that threatened to spill at any moment. But he didn't ask for her sympathy; people rarely did. They just wanted to be heard and understood. She tightened her fingers around his, and their eyes met in the dark. He nodded at her, as though he somehow knew what she was saying, even though she wasn't really sure herself. She understood though, the core of it, the core of him. They were coming from the same place. His sister, in the passenger seat… she'd died right next to him.

They walked in silence for a moment. So this was his story. This was why he loathed going home. She knew that feeling. Everything she used to be comfortable around just reminded her of what she'd lost. Everything had a memory attached, like trying to forge a new path in a forest while the branches from the trees she flattened insisted on swinging back to slap her round the face.

She'd been the one in the driver's seat that day in Sicily, metaphorically speaking. She had waved the guys off, wished them a great fishing trip, told them she'd miss them, all the while planning a large glass of wine or three, a boutique shopping expedition and a gossip session with Nora. The what-ifs never stopped. They hit her when she least expected them, like now, in this cave! What if she'd suggested they listen to the boat-rental guys' warning about the choppy waves instead of agreeing that if they just stuck to the waters around the coast they'd be OK? What if she'd insisted they go tomorrow instead when the weather was due to be better? The guilt she felt, over saying none of those things, and causing Nora to lose her husband, had eaten her up. She would spend the rest of her life making sure Nora was never alone.

Ally was so caught up in her thoughts, she didn't notice the ground in front of her had roughened. Suddenly her foot slipped on the uneven ground, sending small rocks skittering across the cave floor.

'Careful!' Dev's voice came at her sharp as he reached out, his reflexes quick. His hands wrapped around her arms, steadying her before she could fall. The sudden contact sent the mild buzz back up to full-throttle electrifying shockwaves. 'We almost lost you there,' he said, his mouth hitching in one corner.

Pressed against his chest, she felt the steady thump of his heartbeat against her breasts, her lips mere inches from his. His breath came in warm waves against her skin, even warmer for the chill of the cave air, and it sent alarm bells and butterflies raging through her all at once. In that moment, everything else fell away—there was only Dev, the faint scent of soap and damp earth and mosquito repellent and this. Whatever this was.

'We didn't lose me, I'm OK,' she muttered, her voice barely audible over the pounding of her own heart. But she didn't move away, couldn't really, even as her mind screamed at her to put distance between them pronto. The closeness was too comfortable. Comfortably uncomfortable, she contemplated. It was weird and her brain would not compute. She'd placed her womanly cravings into a self-imposed isolation chamber months ago, determined to focus on herself and Nora and Oliver and her career and…and…and it was not enough. Not any more.

Dev's hands remained on her arms, not gripping, not claiming, just there—a silent vow of support that somehow meant more than any words could. She barely knew him, so why did his touch make her feel as she was feeling now? What was it about him?

The air between them crackled. Ally knew she should nip this thing in the bud before it wound any tighter around them and strangled any ounce of professionalism she had left, but then, she had promised Larissa, who apparently was figuring out a fling was also possible in polar climes… In fact, she was probably having freezing-cold sex in an igloo with Thor right at this very moment. Ally's heart was another caveman now, banging on a drum. Raw urgency hummed in the air, and she could almost feel the spirits of a thousand loincloth-wearing men carving a new story on the walls, cheering them on.

Curb your imagination, Ally.

'Ally,' he breathed. The imaginary cavemen went quiet as the slightest brush of his thumb along her forearm sent another pulse of electricity skittering under her skin. Every instinct in her body leaned into his touch.

'Tell me to stop.' Dev's voice was the kind of rough caress that might have come from a scene in an erotic movie. His words, and what they'd just shared, were charging the air between them, second by second.

The word was there, teetering on the edge of her tongue. *Stop.*

The simple command would end this before it went too far and sent her to a place she'd find it very difficult to return from. But because she had always been far too stubborn, even with her own conscience, the word would not come out. Instead, Ally swayed imperceptibly closer, her eyelids fluttering as though they were drawn by the most natural magnetism. For a fleeting second, she allowed herself to believe in the fantasy, that this was a cave of new beginnings! A cave where her delicious fling would begin.

Their breath mingled as Dev tilted his head,

his intent clear in the softening of his deep brown gaze. He was waiting for her to say it. One hundred per cent, it was written all over his face, because right now, he didn't want to stop at all. This close in the half-light, she could see flecks of gold in his eyes, a world of warmth she hadn't noticed before that conversation, or maybe it had been an admission into the world he locked up tight inside his head. Right now it felt as though she could deep-dive into the ocean of Dev and yet never truly discover its depth. Goosebumps erupted across her skin. She submitted entirely to this yo-yo moment—breathless one second and full to bursting with brain-numbing desire the next. *Kiss me, then,* she willed him.

But he didn't.

So *she* would kiss *him*, she decided. Only, as their lips hovered a hair's breadth apart, the hurricane began. It blew in from the back door of her brain and completely decimated the haze of longing that had taken hold of her senses. First she saw her sister's grief-stricken face, pressed into the aeroplane window on the seemingly endless flight back from Sicily, two empty seats where Albie and Matt should've been. Then she heard the nothingness; the hollow echo of loss around Nora's too-quiet house, even as she moved all her stuff in—and she'd had a lot of stuff at the rental she'd shared with Matt. Then the sobbing late at night from the pantry, where Nora locked herself away amongst the tins and the plastic containers, where Oliver couldn't hear her scream. Then her own reflection in the patio doors as she stared at the shed Matt and Albie had put together, while she and Nora had sat there commenting on their work-to-tea-drinking ratio as if they'd had a deadline and were getting paid. Her face pale, her hair, raggedy and unwashed. Her heart, physically aching from her failure to smell Matt on the pillowcase any more. The last of him, the last piece of physical proof of him, gone.

It all surged up from nowhere, or maybe from where she'd stored it for moments like this. A rapid-fire round of harsh reminders came for her, one after the other. This would hurt so badly already, when it ended. With a gasp, Ally jerked back, breaking the spell. She stumbled slightly, her palm leaving the anchor of his chest as she forced the distance between them.

'I—I can't,' she stammered, her voice quivering with a cocktail of emotions that she couldn't fully decipher. 'I mean, stop. We have to stop.'

'We're stopping.' Dev held his hands up high, as though she'd threatened him with a pickaxe.

'Sorry,' she managed to squeeze out, wrapping her arms around herself as though she could hold together all the pieces inside her that felt as if they were about to shatter all over again. What the hell was wrong with her? 'I just—'

'I get it, it's OK,' Dev said, though he looked annoyed, more with himself than with her. His tone was devoid of any anger, which made her feel slightly better but no less ridiculous for over-reacting, both to her memories and to that potential moment of physical connection. 'I got carried away...'

'There's no air in here, it just got to us,' she reasoned, even as the confusion mounted. She hadn't expected that at all, not the almost kiss, not the barrage of memories that had shot in and invoked the fear of God into her. So much for a fling! Maybe she wasn't ready. This attraction to Dev had come at her so suddenly it had thrown everything out of whack, but, realistically, was she even capable?

'We'll just forget all about it,' he said, cementing his own feelings. She tried not to feel disappointed.

Dev dismissed himself to his tent almost as soon as they were back and all night, from her place by the fire, Ally found herself watching his tent, wishing she could just unzip it and crawl inside and curl into him, or at least back into the moment where he'd seen her—all of her, the parts she usually hid away. They had the same pain babbling like a brook under the surface. He was dealing with it differently for sure, but he was still dealing with it. It had united them, created a bond that had turned physical in a heartbeat, it was that strong.

But that kind of pain could never lead to anything except more misery. Misery squared could never equal fun and flings, and she would never risk entering that kind of hellscape again if she could help it.

CHAPTER FIVE

THE AIR IN the coastal village near Kozhikode was as thick as soup, even as the lively Arabian Sea whispered promises of refreshment through the palm fronds. Children giggled in the distance and the less pleasant but ever-present buzz of mosquitoes made Ally scratch her leg on impulse, the second she stepped out of the Jeep after Dev. There was no time for swimming, they had work to do on a new anti-malaria mission. Not that Dev looked in the mood for swimming anyway.

He'd been glued to his phone the whole way here and had hardly uttered a word. Just who he'd been emailing so frantically she had no clue, but he'd worn that look of diligent concentration, almost verging on fiercely unapproachable, that told her she shouldn't ask. They'd barely spoken in over a week. She knew they were both trying to forget what had happened in that cave and all the stuff their admissions had sent shooting back to the surface, but with every day and night that passed they were finding new reasons not to stand or sit close, or to even talk, and it was starting to feel a bit lonely, honestly.

Larry had nothing to offer on it really. Apparently, she'd had a close encounter with Erik, aka Thor, and he'd been weird about it ever since. The compassionate side of Ally wanted to bring it up with Dev, despite the awkwardness of what had almost happened, but the part that didn't want her own backstory of depression and grief to haunt her forced her mouth shut and made her keep her own distance.

Every time she caught him staring off into the distance she wanted to crack a joke, or suggest they explore somewhere else, something new. She wanted the awestruck nerd back, the one who'd smiled and explored those ancient wonders with her, but she hadn't seen that side of Dev since. Almost as if he'd shut some door that she'd started cracking open. Just as she had.

Damn it! Ally smacked at her thigh. Another mosquito bite for the collection—great. Just over three weeks in already, she should be used to the mozzies by now, she thought as Dev shouldered his bag and strode on ahead of her, called by a member of their team, but the constant blotches on her legs were making her feel less human, more pizza, and there was no amount of mosquito repellent that would stop them feasting on her flesh, unfortunately.

Still, this was a different vibe from the vaccine drive. The air hung laden with salt and the tang of fish from the nearby market, and it mingled with the sweet scent of jasmine that was growing in wild abundance along the paths. She was trying to notice the little things now, rather than the big things she'd rather not address, like her mounting crush on the doctor she'd almost kissed in a cave, and the hollow chasm that had opened between them since it happened.

'Namaskaram.' A man with weathered skin and anxious eyes greeted them from a nearby ramshackle building, his hands clasped together in a gesture of respect and urgency. 'We are needing help. Many are sick.'

It struck Ally in this moment, a welcome interruption from her new thinking pattern, which was admittedly mostly about Dev, just how serious a malaria outbreak was with no medical staff or proper facilities. This was exactly why they'd been sent here.

Dev nodded solemnly to the local. His brown eyes swept over the scene, assessing the situation in that calm, methodical way of his that had been driving her crazy ever since she'd seen a glimmer of what must still be swirling underneath. He'd lost his sister. His sister had died a tragic death while *he* was behind the wheel. How could you unsee that, even seven years later? Surely it would haunt you?

'Show us where we can set up,' Dev said, his voice steady. Ally followed suit, trying not to think about the tension that had been building between them since that afternoon. She focused instead on the task at hand, letting the professional mask slide into place on her face, along with a second healthy slather of sunblock, as was becoming standard. They were here to work, she reminded herself, nothing more. Just forget the stupid fling thing. If only she could stop rewinding that magical moment in the cave…before she went and ruined it.

Together, they followed the locals through a maze of narrow lanes, sidestepping chickens and the occasional wandering goat until they reached an open space by the community centre. It was a clearing really, surrounded by houses with terracotta roofs and walls washed in cheery yellows and blues.

'This will do,' Ally declared, her nurse's eye appraising the area for its potential as their triage centre. Dr Anjali Kapur—the Indian physician who'd assigned them to both missions so far— had put her in charge, seeing as staff for this one was limited. She was secretly pleased Dev had been assigned too, though if he hadn't, it might have made things less awkward.

'We need to get organised, fast,' she said, blocking out the way he was still assessing the scene and occasionally her when he didn't think she was looking. She turned to the group from the NHF and directed them with a mix of authority and camaraderie that made it clear she was no stranger to crisis situations, if only they knew. She'd always dreamed of having this much authority. In truth she hadn't been quite sure she could handle it, being used to operations on a smaller scale in Somerset, but this all-hands-on-deck approach to fieldwork was always going to challenge her, shake things up. Wasn't that a part of why she'd applied?

'Let's set up stations for temperature checks here—' she pointed to a shaded spot under a large banyan tree '—and blood tests can be done inside the centre.'

'Right,' said one of the team members, a young lanky guy whose name Ally couldn't quite remember, and he hurried off to unpack the boxes of medical supplies from the back of a second vehicle that had arrived moments after theirs.

'Temperature checks, blood tests…what else?' asked Sameer, their logistics guy, scribbling notes onto a clipboard. Her iPad had died long ago, which reminded her she'd need to source the plug adaptors too.

'Hydration station, rehydration salts…' Dev started.

'We need new mosquito nets, and a rest area for those who've already been seen to,' Ally followed, looking at Sameer now. 'And locate the plug adaptors if you can.'

'Got it,' Sameer replied, hurrying to follow his directives. Ally felt Dev's eyes on her again, but she straightened her face. The fact that people were so willing to follow her caused a buzz of pride to thrill through her as she watched the site spring to life. Maybe she could do this. She rolled her eyes at herself then. She couldn't kiss a guy she was crushing on…but she could do *this*.

Dev was carrying a box, and he watched her over it for a moment with something like admiration flickering in his gaze. Then he masked it with his usual reserved expression, and she bit back a jolt of annoyance. They might not have discussed what happened in the cave but she knew he must still be thinking about it, as she was.

Suddenly a clatter from behind them stole her full attention. Dev dropped the box he was holding and sprinted towards the cause of the commotion: an elderly woman had stumbled and was crouched in a heap on the floor. Ally was beside him in a flash. 'What happened?'

'I don't know,' he said, speaking quickly to

the lady in local dialect while they propped her up between them. 'Make some space, please!' he shouted at the people who were gathering around. Ally ran, retrieved the medical kit and set it down, assessing the scene alongside him.

'Looks like heat exhaustion and dehydration,' Ally diagnosed quickly, checking the woman's pulse, which was weak and rapid. 'Dev, we need to cool her down and rehydrate her immediately. Help me move her to the shade.'

Dev nodded, already positioning himself to assist her. Together they were able to relocate the woman to a cooler spot beneath one of the canopies, where Dev lifted her expertly onto a makeshift exam table. Ally gently tilted the woman's head back to open her airway and checked her breathing. It was shallow.

'We need to lower her body temperature quickly,' she said. As she positioned the woman on her back and elevated her legs on a pile of blankets to encourage blood flow to her vital organs, Dev retrieved a cold pack from the generator-run refrigerator and placed it on the woman's forehead. He then put another under her armpits, while Ally grabbed a third cold pack and pressed it to the back of her neck.

Her hand brushed his and stayed there as together they adjusted the pack under her head. When she caught his eye she swore she could see something burning for her underneath. It felt good to be helping someone with him, knowing they were a trusted team already. This was something she'd never been able to feel with Matt, something that came only from using her training with someone else in the medical field.

'I'll get some water and electrolyte solution ready,' Dev told her as she soothed their patient, who was already doing better for being in the shade, covered in ice packs.

As the woman took small sips of his carefully prepared drink, Dev set up a portable fan and directed it towards Ally, enhancing the cooling effect, and he watched her a moment, the way her hair was blowing around her face, even as she tried to plaster it back. She could feel his eyes on her as he lingered, awaiting more instruction, maybe? 'Her pulse is getting stronger,' she reported, after checking the woman's wrist again.

'Good,' Dev said, the relief evident in his deep voice.

'You go, I'll stay here, and monitor her vitals.'

'You sure?'

Suddenly she felt a little uncomfortable, as if they were back in that cave. 'Yes, I'm sure,' she told him, taking out a blood-pressure cuff and stethoscope from the kit, and busying herself. 'Blood pressure is stabilising, one-ten over seventy.'

Dev nodded approvingly. 'Let me know if you need anything else,' he said, and she purposely did not look at him. It would only make her heart beat harder for him than it already was.

Over the course of the week on site at the camp, Ally lost herself in the rhythm of work, telling her mind that the shared glances with Dev were purely professional as they moved around each other. Every patient who came through their makeshift triage area brought their own story— a grandmother who could barely stand, a father worried for his feverish son, a young woman cradling a listless baby.

Each time Ally's heart broke a little. It was so different here from the clinic, where she'd worked alongside Larissa for five whole years. What would she do after this? She couldn't exactly stay moving about on missions with the NHF—what about Nora, and Oliver? She wanted to go home, eventually.

Dev didn't, which was why he would be the perfect fling—think of all the things they could do around a place like this, all these magical locations to explore together! But no, no way. Her heart might have tugged in his direction for a brief moment but she wasn't cut out for a fling. Her heart loved too hard. And Nora's grief over losing her husband—someone she'd actu-

ally agreed to spend the rest of her life with—
was etched like one of those petroglyphs in her
memory, a chapter in her life that would scar all
of them for as long as they remained breathing.
Imagine losing a husband…worse than a boyfriend. Imagine taking those vows and then having them broken by a cruel twist of fate. It had
put Ally off marriage too. Too much of a risk.

'Next,' she called out, signalling for the next
patient as she readied her thermometer.

Ally wrapped a blood-pressure cuff around the
arm of the middle-aged man who'd taken a seat.
It was the same man who'd greeted them earlier,
she realised. He had selflessly been letting everyone else go before him, till now. His skin was
slick with sweat from fever. The line of villagers
still waiting for medical attention seemed to be
growing rather than shrinking.

'Started about two weeks ago,' the man murmured, his voice weak. 'First it was just a few
cases. Then, before we knew it, everyone was
falling sick. We sent word to NHF when we realised we couldn't manage alone.'

'Thank you for letting us know,' Ally replied
soothingly. 'We're here to help, and we will, OK?
As many people as we can.' She offered a reassuring smile, even as her mind raced with the
gravity of the situation. If not contained, the out-

break could ravage the entire village. It seemed bad enough already.

Another commotion at the edge of their triage tent drew her attention. A young man had stumbled in, clutching his side and grimacing in pain. It wasn't malaria, she could tell that already. Dev shot her a look that said he'd deal with it, and she joined him after a few minutes, unable to ignore the cries of pain.

'Possible appendicitis,' Dev concluded after a quick assessment, his eyes meeting hers.

'Let's get him comfortable,' she said, already moving to fetch pain relievers and prepare an IV. Working alongside Dev, she found their movements fell into a familiar dance. It hadn't been long, working together like this in these remote locations, but somehow each step they took seemed to anticipate the other's needs. He was impressive, that much was for sure. She'd bet it almost destroyed him, when his sister died right next to him, knowing there was probably nothing he could have done. She had been a little selfish not bringing it up again, she thought now. He hadn't shared much, but that should have been enough!

Maybe she should try and talk to him again...

As Dev's hands skilfully guided the needle into the patient's vein, Ally caught herself watching him closely—his brow furrowed in concentration, a bead of sweat trailing down his temple. It reminded her of the vulnerability they had shared in that moment, right before their lips almost touched. He'd be an excellent kisser. The way he concentrated so deeply on everything he did.

She shook her head, refocusing on the task at hand. She would talk to him. That was all. No more kissing. Or getting close to kissing. It was not going to happen.

'Thank you,' their patient managed now through clenched teeth as the pain medication took effect.

'We need to get you to the hospital,' Dev told the young guy gently. 'You'll be OK.'

'I'm on it.' Ally made the call and Dev took over, his hands finding hers over the IV and sending a spark of adrenaline through her veins.

'They'll be here in half an hour. It's the best we can do from here,' she said.

Dev nodded sagely and asked her to bring some more water. She did so gladly. She would follow any instruction he gave her, she realised. They made a good team. The trust had been there from the start. Well, on a professional level anyway. She didn't trust the way her heart revved up every time they worked together like this or whenever else they were close.

Dev's eye for everyone else's well-being never faltered, and she wondered if he'd chosen this profession, or at least this constant string of as-

signments far away from Toronto, to somehow
assuage his obvious guilt for whatever happened
that night, with his sister. If he was helping other
people, he was doing what he couldn't have done
for his sister.

Just as she was doing what Matt would have
been proud of *her* for doing, she thought with a
pang. It was no longer a pang of missing him,
she realised suddenly, eyes on Dev's broad back.
More a pang of recognition that she was moving on, and that, since being here, things were
undoubtedly brighter than they had been even a
few months ago. Even if she still couldn't seem
to kiss anyone, Well…specifically Dev, who was
so much like her it was actually scary.

'Ally?' Someone's voice pulled her from her
thoughts. 'Can you check on Mrs Kumar? I think
she's ready for another round of antimalarials.'

The sun dipped lower and dazzled in the palm
fronds as the last few patients were seen to. Ally's muscles ached from the continuous work, and
her mosquito bites itched like mad, but at least
the team were making a difference here, however
small it might seem. Their appendicitis patient
was doing fine in the hospital, and she found
herself thinking about him as she stepped over
the threshold of another temporary abode, hun-
gry and exhausted. They'd worked fast, she and

Dev, almost on autopilot. What would their kisses be like, if they could read each other this way?

The small house, which was serving as a guest house to herself and one other NHF worker who had yet to arrive, was a quaint structure with whitewashed walls and a terracotta-tiled roof. Her hosts, a middle-aged couple whose smiles were as warm as the chai they offered her, watched in amusement as she pushed strands of hair back behind her ears and let them show her to her room. It was unfortunate that they stayed only a few days in each place unless they were on a campsite, but the NHF didn't want to invade local communities for long, for various reasons, and at least she was meeting lots of lovely people.

'Your hair is like fire,' the hostess said as Ally put her bag down on the bed. 'Very funny!'

'Thanks, I think,' Ally replied, offering them a smile. She was used to standing out with her auburn hair, but the amusement it brought to others here in India never failed to amuse *her*.

The symphony of insects outside made a lulling melody as the hosts chatted to her in broken English. Ally was being polite. All she wanted to do was call Larry for an update on her own assignment and Thor, then pass out on the bed.

Her room was charmingly modest. A standing fan whirred rhythmically from one corner, sending a breeze across the four-poster bed, which thankfully had mosquito netting draped across its frame. Not that there was much room on her body for any more bites. A single bulb hanging from the ceiling cast warm shadows over three vibrant paintings depicting local life on the walls. One had a goat on it.

'Is that your doctor kit?' a small voice piped up from the doorway. A boy peered in with curiosity and was quickly introduced by her hosts as Anish, their young son. He had a mop of curly black hair and his big brown eyes widened with intrigue as he danced up to her and peered into her bag.

'Part of it, yes,' Ally answered, lowering it to show him properly, impressed by his English. The kids spoke it better than the adults. She pulled out a stethoscope, its metal parts gleaming in the soft light. 'This helps me listen to hearts.'

'Can I hear mine?' Anish asked.

'Sure.' She placed the ear tips gently into his ears and guided the chest piece to his left pectoral. 'Breathe normally.'

Anish's face lit up with wonder as the sound of his heartbeat filled his ears. His small chest swelled with pride, and Ally pictured eight-year-old Oliver again, the way his face always lit up when she walked into the house. She was glad every time she could bring a smile to his cute face, and sometimes wondered how many memories he'd retain of his dad, if any. He was only six when he passed. Still, he was a spirited kid. Oliver always puffed out his chest when he felt important and involved over something small, just as Anish was doing now.

'I want to help!'

'Maybe you can be my assistant later,' Ally teased. He was so cute, and his enthusiasm was endearing as she continued to unpack, arranging bandages, antimalarials and diagnostic tools on a nearby antique dresser, partly so she could double-check she'd have everything she might need for an emergency anywhere, any time, partly so Anish could feel involved.

Soon she heard the front door creaking open again, and her hosts greeting someone else. Then…oh, no.

Dev stopped at her door, his silhouette framed by the light from another low-hanging bulb, registering it was her immediately. Her heart started thudding like an old clock in her chest.

'Looks like we're neighbours,' he commented, his voice betraying nothing of the tension that hummed between them like one giant cloud of mosquitoes.

Of course, it would be you.

His dark hair was tousled, and there was a hint of weariness in the lines around his brown eyes that matched her own. They'd both been flat out all day.

'It's a cute place, isn't it?' she responded, letting her gaze flicker away as she busied herself with the equipment again. 'You must be exhausted.'

'Long day,' he said, simply.

She could feel his proximity like static in the air until he cleared his throat, shifting his weight from one foot to the other, his rucksack still slung over his shoulder. She almost asked if they could talk. They needed to talk, she felt so bad that they'd just left things like this, and so must he. But something stopped her.

'I'll just, uh, settle in next door, then,' he said.

'Right,' Ally murmured, her hands suddenly clumsy with the book she was holding. She didn't dare look up again. Eye contact would most definitely unravel the facade she'd somehow constructed. Thankfully Anish bounded over to him and asked if he could see his bag too. She soon heard the kid chatting in Hindi with Dev in the room next door. Dev sounded extra hot when he spoke Hindi.

Alone again, Ally released a massive breath she hadn't even realised she'd been holding in. The tightness in her chest eased a bit but underneath it all, the worry gnawed at her—they couldn't go on like this. And how the heck was she supposed to keep her calls to Larry about him quiet enough for Dev not to hear? As if reading her mind, her phone buzzed. She clutched at it.

'Larissa!'

'Hey, how's it going? Any news on Dev the delicious?'

Ally paused, then lowered her voice and told her she didn't think a fling was going to be possible, that there was just too much going on with the workload and the heat and her body full of mosquito bites. Larissa filled her in on the dog she'd been walking every morning, and how Thor had bought her some ridiculously expensive imported strawberries and how she really needed to start reading *A Court of Thorns and Roses*. Ally listened, still mentally going over her encounters with Dev 'the delicious'. She could barely even talk to the guy any more, so caught up in her head was she. And how was she meant to sleep at all, knowing he was in the bed right next door? This mission had just got a lot more complicated.

CHAPTER SIX

DEV PRESSED HIS back to the rickety headboard under the whirring ceiling fan. Another email with the emboldened subject line *Valentine's Day* glared up at him from his phone screen. His brother, Romesh, had written again this morning, after he'd failed to respond to Mom. They all wanted an answer. Was he coming home this year or not? Because he'd missed last year, and the one before, and they really wanted to do something special as a family in Roisin's memory. Neither had said what, but Mom was hinting that she'd tell him in a call. It was a ploy to get him to call her, and it sent the guilt into slasher mode inside his brain.

His thumb hovered over the keyboard as indecision gnawed at him from all angles. It wasn't the logistics holding him back from agreeing to fly back to Toronto; he could plan assignments with the NHF around anything and his role was well cemented now, enabling him to drop in and out of location-based projects wherever he liked.

It was the thought of being sucked back into the maelstrom of regret and grief and guilt that made him reluctant even to answer these emails.

They'd never said it, but they all knew he'd taken a different route that night, and that he'd failed to persuade her to put the seat belt back on when Roisin had been tipsy and belligerent and had cheekily unbuckled it to try and reach for his bag in the back seat, where the bottle of rum from the party they'd just left had still been sloshing about. If he'd just ignored her drunken chiding and kept his eyes on the road...

Dev was deep in thought, rereading the message for the tenth time, just as a groan cut through the quiet house. He was on his feet before he even registered moving, instinct taking over as he strode down the hallway towards the sound. In seconds, another groan led him to young Anish. He was doubled over in the bathroom.

'Anish?' Dev knelt beside the boy quickly, touching a hand to his back. The child was obviously distressed, and sick.

Anish looked up, his face pale and sheened with sweat, his eyes glassy with pain. 'It hurts,' he gasped, clutching his stomach.

'Where does it hurt, buddy?' Dev coaxed him to lie down on the floor. Quickly but calmly he assessed the boy's abdomen, feeling for distension or abnormal rigidity. This had come on fast. It was possibly food poisoning.

'Here,' Anish moaned, pressing on his mid-section.

Dev noted the signs—this seemingly acute onset of abdominal pain, the nausea, the cold clamminess of his skin. When Anish opened his mouth to groan again, Dev caught the sour scent of vomit, just as he saw it spattered on the toilet and floor. It all confirmed his suspicions. Gastro-enteritis. It wasn't uncommon here, but in a child this young, it could turn dangerous fast without proper care.

'OK, Anish, don't worry, we're going to make this stop for you,' Dev said, mentally cataloguing the steps he'd need to take—hydration, electro-lyte replacement, monitoring for signs of further dehydration. All doable, even here in the mid-dle of the night. Luckily he and Ally had both brought their medical supplies from the camp. Ally, he thought with a frown. He'd have to wake her.

'Will you make it stop hurting?' Anish's voice was small but Dev caught a flicker of trust through the pain that sent his mind back to Nikki, the day his nephew had grazed both knees falling off a cannon at the play park's castle, and he'd patched him up. That was the last time he'd been home. He might be a decent uncle from time to time but, to Nikki and Romesh, it wasn't enough.

Suddenly his attention snapped from the groaning boy to the soft padding of footsteps. Ally emerged, her pale blue oversized T-shirt clinging to her in a way that was both innocent and inadvertently seductive. Oh, man. Dev's throat went dry on the spot, making him clear it louder than he'd intended. He quickly averted his eyes, hoping his professionalism covered the twist of attraction towards her inside him. It was still there, simmering between them like a watched pot that neither was allowing to boil over, and how could he, after she'd sprung away from him in the cave like that?

'Anish?' she whispered now, her voice thick with sleep and concern.

'Ally, could you—?' Dev began, but she was already moving past him, her nurse's instincts kicking in as she assessed the situation. He told her his suspicions and she agreed, racing for her supplies. She barely met his eyes though, and he couldn't help a glimmer of annoyance seeping in, maybe because he was so tired, maybe because she looked so hot in that T-shirt and he could do absolutely nothing about it.

Anish's mother was here now, looking concerned to say the least.

'Mrs Kapoor, why don't you rest in the sitting

room? We'll look after Anish,' Ally suggested gently on her way back in. For a moment the boy's mother just hovered at the bathroom door, wringing her hands. But she allowed Ally to help her to the couch next door.

He watched her while he stilled the boy and pressed a damp towel to his head. Before that near kiss, Ally had been giving him all the signs, in fact, he'd been so certain she wanted it…but right at the last minute she'd thought better for some reason. Maybe she wasn't over her dead boyfriend. Probably for the best she stopped it, he thought, and had thought many times since. She was as damaged as he was, that much was evident. And she didn't even know that he had sworn he wouldn't go there with another team member after Cassinda. He'd almost broken his vow to himself.

Still, the tension that had lingered between them seemed to dissolve as they saw to Anish on the bathroom floor, where it was at least cool. They worked in tandem, Ally helping the boy to the toilet to be sick again, and cleaning him up, while Dev measured out an antiemetic.

'Small sips, Anish. It'll help with the nausea,' Dev coaxed, explaining what he was saying in Hindi instead of offering the kid English, as Ally had to. She watched him offering a spoon-ful of the medication to the boy's lips, and he didn't miss her T-shirt bunched up accidentally higher on one thigh as she bent across the bath to fetch another towel, revealing the soft white flesh speckled with swollen red mounds from the insect bites.

'Thank you, Doctor,' Anish mumbled.

'This is my job, champ. Let's get you feeling better.'

As the hours crept by, they took turns wiping Anish's clammy forehead with a cool cloth and Ally told him stories in English, which made him smile through his fever. Eventually he felt OK about moving to the sitting room with his mother and Ally prepared the oral rehydration salts, showing Anish's mother how to do it, too.

'Looks like someone's finally turned a corner,' Ally said some time later as Anish's breathing evened out. The cramps that had racked his small body were indeed finally easing.

'Thanks for getting up in the middle of the night,' Dev said, catching her pale blue eyes in the dim light, forcing his eyes not to travel down her T-shirt to her bare legs and feet, or over the curve of her breasts. She nodded and he pretended he hadn't been glancing at her chest, because she wasn't wearing a bra.

Dawn crept up on them as they settled Anish back into bed. His mother was still fast asleep on the couch, exhausted from worry. Together, they tucked the sheets around the boy. Watching Ally smooth back Anish's hair, Dev couldn't help but think she'd make a great parent one day. He'd figured out by now of course that she was an aunt, not a mother, but her compassion and warmth shone through in the smallest actions, all day, everywhere they went, and he knew she'd be the kind of doting mother who would do anything for their child. Like his own, he thought with a pang.

Outside on the porch, only the chatter of insects and the melodic call of a lone koel filled the air. Dev leaned against the wooden railing, letting out a long, tired sigh, rubbing his eyes against the grittiness of sleep deprivation. Glancing back at the still house, he pondered over that email glowing on his phone's screen like an omen. The thought of re-entering that world twisted in his gut.

His parents had never moved house since arriving in Canada, so he'd have to take the small childhood bedroom he'd slept in next to Roisin's. Mom wouldn't dream of him staying in a hotel. She always wanted them all close for the occasion. Even Romesh and his wife and Nikki had to stay there, in an awkward set-up in his old bedroom, which was now an extension of his father's home office.

'Here.' Ally's voice cut through his reverie as

she stepped outside into the dawn light that was now starting to spill onto the porch. She handed him a steaming mug of coffee.

'Thanks,' Dev managed, accepting it with a grateful nod. The warmth from the cup seeped into his hands, grounding him. 'You've changed.'

'No, I'm the same person.' Ally's mouth shifted to the side, as if she was judging whether to actually laugh at her own joke. She glanced down at herself in the comfortable top and shorts she'd swapped her oversized T-shirt for. 'Sorry. Yeah, I didn't think anyone needed to see any more of my sleepwear,' she said, and he stopped himself saying anything at all.

'I hope he's gonna be OK,' she said with a sigh, bobbing her head back towards the house and pressing the mug to her mouth. It took his mind right back to almost kissing her.

'He will.'

'And I hope it doesn't spread. He reminds me of Oliver when he's sick.' Ally perched herself on the edge of a wicker chair. 'He gets this little crease between his brows, just like Anish. Mind you, most kids remind me of Oliver.'

'Your nephew, right?' Dev questioned, despite knowing the answer.

'My nephew.' She smiled, though her eyes carried a twinge of pain that drew him closer to her instantly, like a magnet. 'Family's so important, you know?' She pulled a face in his direction. 'Oh, sorry, I didn't mean… I mean…'

'It's OK,' he said. As she spoke, Ally absent-mindedly scratched at her arms. The reddened welts from her mosquito bites stood out against her skin even in the soft light and Dev made a mental note; he had a remedy for that, or at least an old healer in the village did, not far from here. He'd met her on his first assignment several years ago, when she'd brought him several natural remedies he'd been unsure of at the start, all of which went on to help heal his patients in various ways. He'd take her there tomorrow.

'I miss my nephew too,' he admitted now. 'Nikki is my brother Romesh's first, and only.'

'Are you close with your brother?' she asked.

He shook his head slowly. 'Used to be. He, Roisin and I were inseparable growing up. Nikki was barely two when she died, so he didn't even get to know his aunt.'

Why was he telling her all this? Dev rolled his mug between his hands, feeling the warmth seep into his skin, allowing the bitter liquid to battle his fatigue. It wasn't worth going back to bed now. They had to be back at the site soon. He was grateful for the silence now, for the momentary peace it always offered before the world woke up, but Ally was still looking at him. He knew they should probably bring up what had happened between them just over a week ago, and he could tell she sort of wanted to, too.

'I had an email from my mother, and then one from my brother,' he found himself saying instead, on an exhale he hadn't known was building in his chest. 'Mom wants me to go home to Toronto. There's a family thing every year in honour of Roisin on her birthday. Feb fourteenth.'

'Valentine's Day.' Ally tilted her head, the soft curls of her auburn hair brushing against her shoulders. 'And you don't want to go, do you? Because of the memories.'

He turned to her, wondering what was making him divulge all this, suddenly. Maybe because he had no one else to talk to, and she was here. Maybe because she was the one person who might understand.

'I haven't been in three years. It's so selfish, isn't it?' he said, tracing the rim of the mug with his thumb. 'They say they all want me there, but I just don't know how that can be true…'

'Why? Why wouldn't that be true?' she asked, her eyebrows knitting together. She fixed him with that pale blue gaze that always seemed to see more of him than he wanted her to, all things considered. He shouldn't want this woman as much as he was starting to want her. She'd asked him to stop, and he'd stopped, but here he was, telling her all this.

The silence dragged on as they sipped their drinks, watching a hummingbird flit up to the feeder dangling on its string from the overhang.

'I felt the same around my sister for a while,' Ally said, after a beat. 'Like, maybe I shouldn't be there. Just seeing her swollen eyes and her red nose, and hearing her talking to Oliver, explaining why his dad wouldn't be coming back. I thought it was my fault. Like I could have done something to stop them from going out on that boat. We knew the weather was forecast to be bad…' She stopped herself, pressing her mug to her chest. 'If only I'd stopped them going. But how were we to know what would happen? They both *wanted* to go.'

'The boat capsized?' he asked gently, and she nodded softly as his heart started pounding at the thought of it. Her boyfriend, and her sister's husband. So tragic.

'They found them that same night. We were on holiday in Sicily, so nowhere near home. But… my point is, Nora felt the same as me. She also blamed herself for not stopping them. In the end, we could have spent our lives blaming ourselves, or band together and do what was best for Oliver. This is the first time I've left them.'

Dev felt the weight of her words settle over him like a blanket, warm but suffocating all at once. Without thinking, he reached out, briefly touching her arm. It was a simple gesture of solidarity, but it instantly took him back to that cave, and a hot whip lanced his stomach. He stepped back slightly, putting some distance between them. She did the same quickly, sipped on her coffee, then put her mug down and turned to him. Their eyes met and something unspoken passed between them—a recognition of these shared insecurities? It was so strange, the things that kept bringing them together. They still hadn't addressed the last time. Not with words. She stepped even closer, and he mirrored her, moving towards her again.

'Ally,' he began, setting his own cup down, realising his voice was barely louder than the hum of the insects now, 'what happened last week. I think—'

The words caught in his throat as she closed what was left of the space between them, and her lips found his. It started softly, a parting of their lips, a gentle brush, like a test. Then he went back for more, keeping his forehead pressed to hers a moment, running his tongue against hers, till a small groan made its way up his throat and into his mouth, sending her hands to his face, drawing him closer.

The next kiss was loaded with desire, all tongues and hands and heated breath from both, but as quickly as it started, Ally pulled back, training a finger across her lips, as if she was regretting it again. No. There was no way he was letting her do *that* again, not now he'd tasted this and felt her physical response to him and heard her say all that. He reached for her again and her arms looped around his back and shoulders as if refinding her place against his body was as natural as breathing. Something about her was so familiar, he couldn't even place it. Maybe he shouldn't try.

His hands found the curve of her waist through her clothes. 'Are you sure?' he whispered against her lips, just in case.

She pulled back slightly so her hips were barely brushing his, and pressed her palm to his cheek. 'It was just a kiss,' she said with an element of finality and determination that threw him off track for a moment. '*Just* a kiss.'

'If you say so.'

Her eyes narrowed, and she threw her gaze sideways, as if she was coming to some agreement with herself more than with him. 'I do. I do say so,' she said. 'But it doesn't mean I won't require more of them.'

He grinned, despite himself, finding her waist again. 'OK.'

The sound of Anish's mother stirring in the house caught his ears. Footsteps coming towards the porch made Ally jump backwards. 'More coffee?' the woman asked, looking between them, oblivious.

'No, thank you,' they said at the same time, and, with her head held high, Ally excused herself and headed past her, back to her room, leaving him reeling.

CHAPTER SEVEN

THE BUZZ OF conversation filled the local community centre. Ally stood at the front, scratching her arms, scanning the crowd of local leaders and residents who had gathered to receive the new supplies. Beside her, Dev's presence was a grounding force, his tall frame and dark, intent gaze adding weight to the gravity of this joint mission. She was probably on dangerous ground with her colleague after that kiss, but, as she'd said, it was just a kiss. Nothing to get hung up on. Nothing she would miss too much when it ended. Nothing that could ever cause her world to come crashing back down.

So why did her blood skitter to parts she wished it wouldn't, every time he looked at her? Before they'd left this morning, she'd sat at the table with Anish, who thankfully was doing much, much better, and Dev had sat opposite, brushing his foot against hers underneath it on purpose. She hadn't been able to look at him in case she gave the game away to Anish and his mother, who had been so lovely to them so far. It wouldn't do to come off as unprofessional, using her place for a casual hook-up. That wasn't what this was. Or was it? Her mind flickered back to the porch before they'd been interrupted, how he'd looked at her. A rush of warmth flooded her cheeks and she shoved the thought away, refocusing on the crowd.

'Good evening, everyone,' she started, making sure her voice was clear and steady. She was his colleague, someone he could rely on, above anything else, she reminded herself, forcing the thought of his lips on hers away yet again. She'd tasted that kiss all morning, taken a part of him into her bloodstream after learning all that about his family, too. 'We're going to show you the latest supplies, and hand out some mosquito nets. Please come forward if you need them, and, of course, feel free to ask us any questions!'

Dev translated, as he'd taken to doing when Priya, the actual translator, was busy with the patients elsewhere, which was most of the time. They were here to detail the risks posed by malaria and the facts they all really needed to know. As people approached for their nets and sprays, Dev chimed in with some statistics and personal anecdotes from his work in various other places, painting a vivid picture of some of the communities he'd visited on his travels during the last six or seven years he'd been with the NHF. Avoiding going home as much as possible.

After this morning, she was starting to understand a little more where he was coming from with that decision, but she'd pretty much gathered that he blamed himself for what had clearly been an accident. The details hadn't exactly been spelled out, but it was obvious. Her heart had practically spun upside down as she'd told him about herself and Nora, how they'd both blamed themselves for a while for what had happened with the guys. Sometimes, she still did, she thought, suddenly feeling far too far away from her sister again. But whether her point had sunk in, she couldn't tell. She'd been too busy throwing herself on him.

Every time Dev spoke, his deep voice resonated around the crowd in a way that made her skin prickle for him, like a starved cactus calling for water. What had she started? He was talking about mosquito nets, for goodness' sake, and she *still* wanted to jump him.

But the people here were so grateful and kind, which filled her with pride for both herself and Dev. It was good to know their work here wasn't going unnoticed. Good to feel useful. A few people even approached the front, their arms extended with home-made treats and tokens of their gratitude, their smiles wide and genuine.

'Your being here is a blessing to our families,' one elder lady said to her when they'd called break time. Ally didn't quite know what to say as the woman placed a woven basket filled with ripe mangoes on the floor at her feet.

'Thank you,' she managed, her heart swelling on the spot. She glanced at Dev, catching him observing her with that unreadable expression he sometimes got stuck on his face. Was it admiration? Yes…she believed it was. It made her pulse quicken, even as she was swept away by someone else and their questions.

As the area slowly emptied of its occupants, the air buzzed with energised chatter and Ally caught Dev's gaze from across the room, where he was speaking with the elder who'd given them fruit. His eyes were on her again and she didn't miss a glint of something more than just professional admiration shimmering in their depths. Was he talking about her? She realised she had butterflies, or maybe giant mosquitoes, in her belly. It was a look that said he saw her—not just Ally, the nurse, but Ally, the woman who had been through the same spin cycle of horror, devastation and guilt that he had…and whose lips still tingled and burned for more of the same connection. Even if a part of them knew they'd never forget what it was exactly that connected them so deeply. It wasn't the best foundation, but it meant something.

Oh, gosh, are you getting in over your head already? Calm down, Ally! You were determined for it to mean nothing.

'Looks like we have mangoes for life,' Dev said, approaching her once the last of the villagers had trickled out. She looked down to their gift and moved it to a nearby table to take back to the guest house, before finding her eyes drawn back to his lips.

It meant nothing, she reminded herself firmly, scratching a sudden itch above her knee. *It was just a kiss,* just as she'd told him.

She was here to have a fling. If only these damn mozzies would stop trying to eat her alive in the process.

'All we need is a blender. I make a mean smoothie. Oliver loves them,' she told him, forcing a smile to her face as she felt another pang for her sweet nephew. Was he missing her yet?

Dev stepped towards her, 'I don't have a blender. But I do have something else I think you'll appreciate.'

Ally forced her smile into a look that she hoped represented indifference and probably failed as her stomach lurched at his words. It felt like their secret was coming loose at the seams, leaving trails in the breeze for everyone to pick up. She tucked a loose strand of hair behind her ear.

'Come with me,' he said, his voice low and laced with a hint of intrigue that sent a ripple of anticipation down her spine.

She followed him, her curiosity piqued, as they navigated through the NHF workers clearing up and into a secluded alcove behind the community centre. The walls felt as though they were cocooning them in a world far away from their responsibilities and she couldn't suppress her grin as, without warning, Dev's hands cupped her cheeks, and he closed the distance between them. The kiss was a firestorm of suppressed longing breaking free and she gasped. His lips moved against hers with an urgency that made her pulse shoot straight to her groin, and the world faded into insignificance.

'I've been wanting to do that all day,' he breathed against her mouth, his fingers threading through her hair.

'Just another kiss?' she whispered, and she felt his smile spread under her lips.

'Just another kiss,' he replied, drawing her in as she grabbed him by the front of his shirt. He'd long given up on buttoning it up all the way to top, it was just too hot. Hot, hot, *hot*. Their attraction was magnetic, undeniable, she thought as their tongues danced and twirled together. She'd thrown up so many cautious walls around herself since Matt died and now she was coming back to life.

As long as she didn't get carried away. Her heart would not at any point get involved in whatever this was. Fun, it was fun, she reminded herself as Dev's arms wrapped around her harder, pulling her closer. This felt too good. Dangerously good. Her heart was dancing the samba as what felt like an hour later—but was probably only a couple of minutes later—he gently disentangled himself, his eyes sparkling with something mischievous that forced an internal groan to echo throughout her entire body.

'I almost forgot, I have a cure for those itchy mosquito bites you've been complaining about,' he said, a grin tugging at the corner of his mouth as she buffed up her hair. 'It involves a little diversion.'

'Is that so?' she replied, scepticism lacing her tone, though she couldn't suppress the flutter in her stomach. She should probably not take any diversions from her duties, neither big nor little, but then they were done for the day, besides the paperwork, which could be dealt with later.

'Trust me,' he said, leading her away from the community centre and onto a forest trail at the back. The funny thing was, she did. The idea of a little dalliance with Dev was exciting. And he'd thought about her mosquito bites too… Talk about a hero.

They hurried the last few steps to avoid being seen. The sunlight played peekaboo through the dense canopy above and the silence kicked in, nothing but their footsteps and the sounds of insects and birds. As they walked, he stopped occasionally, pulling her into his arms for another intoxicating kiss. Each one sent her heart into overdrive. Oh, my…she couldn't wait to tell Larissa how into it he was.

Ally felt giddy, like a schoolgirl with a secret crush, relishing the illicit thrill of this secret escapade. Larissa was going to melt. She was likely frozen in place, what with her current location…not that Thor, aka Erik, wasn't thawing her out being hotter than Iceland's volcanic craters. Good, Larry deserved some fun, too.

Soon they reached a clearing, and Ally felt her eyes widen at the sight of a small camp nestled unassumingly in the protection of the forest. A tent constructed of worn and faded canvas stood right in the centre, and an older woman with silver hair in braids emerged. She regarded them with knowing eyes that seemed to see right through Ally and, for some reason, Ally felt nervous.

'Um…' she started, but Dev was already approaching the woman, reaching out a hand.

'This is Amrita,' he introduced. Amrita looked to be about ninety-nine years old. In the light, Ally saw the lines of wisdom etched into her skin and she was instantly humbled. 'We met a few years ago on an assignment nearby.'

Inside her tent, the air was thick and stuffy in a good way with the scent of herbs and spices, all mingling with the unmistakable aroma of incense. It was more like a pharmacy and it was clear that this was no pop-up arrangement. Rows of glass bottles lined the shelves, filled with contents of every hue—amber liquids, powders in every shade imaginable, and more jars of unidentifiable balms.

'Everything is made from what's around here, what grows wild,' Dev explained, picking up a small vial that was filled with a vibrant green paste. 'This is made from neem leaves, for example—it's really good for skin irritations.'

Ally peered closer at a jar containing a honey-coloured syrup. How did he know all this stuff? 'And this one?'

'That's a cough remedy, I think, with wild honey and tulsi leaves.' He came up so close behind her that she could feel his breath on the back of her neck, and instantly she felt warmer herself. It was very impressive that he knew all this stuff. Amrita was chiming in, her eyes twinkling as Dev translated. 'She says it's especially good in the monsoon season.'

Each potion seemed more intriguing than the last, and Dev explained that Amrita was a healer, a keeper of ancient wisdom that transcended the modern medicine they both practised in the western world. Ally couldn't help but imagine this woman sitting in a wicker chair in the corner of her sterile clinic back in Frome, dishing out her little vials and jars.

'Here we are, here's what we came for,' Dev said now, offering Ally a tiny bottle that Amrita had given him. 'Try this. It's a blend of citronella and eucalyptus oils. A natural mosquito repellent. It's pretty strong, better than anything you'll get in the pharmacy back home.'

Ally expressed her thanks, taking the bottle, and she felt his eyes on her as she dabbed a bit of the oil onto her pulse points, inhaling the sharp, clean scent. He handed her another, told her to rub it on her bites, and the cool liquid on her skin tingled. The sense of relief was immediate, and she let out a long sigh, surprised to find her eyes were damp.

'I didn't even know how much I needed this. Thank you,' she whispered.

In this moment, the connection she felt to this place and these people stretched beyond the physical and into something far more. It felt a lot like something her soul had been needing, without her even knowing. She could picture Larissa standing in the tent doorway, saying something like, 'See, you wanted an adventure! How about this for an adventure?'

Desperate for more of the pleasant tingling to override the itching on her shoulder blade, she tried to reach a new itch. 'Let me help with that,' Dev offered. Dev's presence in the tent seemed to take up more space than physically possible all of a sudden, especially with Amrita looking on.

'Um, there's more light outside?' she managed, edging towards the doorway. Quickly she stepped back out into the sun, where she could breathe.

'Where?' he asked.

'You'll see it,' she replied, the word barely above a whisper, as she turned her back to him. She gathered her hair and swept it over one shoulder, exposing the nape of her neck and the expanse of skin down her back that she couldn't quite reach.

His fingers brushed against her skin as he uncapped the bottle, sending a shiver down her spine. The potion was cool as it touched her inflamed bites, but it was Dev's touch that ignited a roaring fire inside her. His hands were gentle yet firm, the movements deliberate as he spread the remedy across her skin. Ally closed her eyes, noting how the sensation of his touch was somehow both soothing and intoxicating at the same time. Instantly she was picturing his hands going everywhere else, and she would let them, she realised, feeling wicked.

Opening her eyes, she saw Amrita had stepped outside. She clenched her palms at her sides, so they wouldn't reach for Dev. She wouldn't touch him.

'Does that feel better?' he murmured close to her ear, his breath fanning over her shoulder.

'Much,' she managed to say.

'Good. Because it all feels good to me,' he said softly.

Oh, my goodness.

They could start a fire, she thought, swallowing back a retort before she landed herself in trouble.

'Your remedies are wonderful,' she said quickly to Amrita, willing the flush to vacate her cheeks. Did Amrita hear the way Dev had just been flirting with her? She'd come here to work, she'd promised Nora and Oliver she would be working, not…having a good time?

Why couldn't she have a good time? Because the need to merely soldier onwards was all she'd known for way too long, and she didn't quite know how to live properly in the moment just yet, she realised. And also, she missed home.

The old woman studied Ally with eyes that

118 NURSE'S KERALAN TEMPTATION

seemed to pierce right through her. 'Child, there's a sadness around you,' she observed suddenly. Then she said something else in Hindi to Dev that for some reason made her heart start to rev like a rusty engine.

Dev translated, screwing the lid back on the potion. Half smiling, and sort of frowning, he turned to her. 'She said your sorrow is like clouds before the rain.'

Ally's heart jumped to the tip of her tongue. How could this near stranger see what was going on inside her head?

'She wants to know if we'll join her for a blessing ceremony,' Dev told her, letting the old woman squeeze his hands.

A what? she wanted to say, picturing herself in the back of that yin yoga class she'd dragged Larissa to not so long ago, when they'd had to sit on tennis balls with their hands in the heart position for so long she'd had a tennis-ball-sized bruise on her bum for two weeks after.

Dev was looking at her with that intent look he probably mastered at birth, probably noting her scepticism. She heard Larissa again in her head, reminding her she was here for adventure.

'OK,' Ally said. 'Sure, let's do it.'

Ally lay on the mat looking up at the sky. It was made of woven grass, and it was making her thighs itch more than the mosquito bites, but the earth beneath her was cool under the forest canopy, a much-needed respite from the heat of the sun. Hopefully someone was looking out for leopards.

The scent of incense curled through the air, mingling with the musk of the fauna, and Amrita's rhythmic, soothing voice seemed to harmonise with the distant calls of the birds and the chirping bugs. If only Ally could bottle this and import it to Somerset, where the stench of cow manure and the sound of churning tractor wheels were prevalent over anything else, most of the time.

She closed her eyes as the ceremony—whatever it was supposed to achieve—began, letting the chant wash over her like a gentle wave. Dev lay on the mat beside her. She opened her eyes to look at him. Surprisingly, he was immersed in the moment. OK, then, maybe there was something in this, she thought. Maybe it wouldn't leave her jaded to all things spiritual as that tennis ball in the yin yoga class did.

The ritual turned out to be quite profound, involving a series of chants in Hindi and low mutterings in no language at all, the burning of herbs, and the laying of hands. As Amrita's palms hovered above her, Ally felt an unexpected warmth radiating through her belly, right around her heart. Confused, she opened her eyes again, but there was no fire, nothing hot at all. Weird.

The heat seeped deeper into her pores, and the longer she had her eyes shut, the more she felt it melting away some of the heaviness that had cocooned around her. She'd known it was there, of course, but somehow only now, as it dissipated, did she realise how much darkness had been there since Albie and Matt died, and…oh, gosh, poor Nora. If only Nora could be here, too, she thought.

Now it was as if each intonation untangled a knot inside her, unravelling the grief in some way and leaving room for breath, for life. She was surprised to find hot tears pricking the backs of her eyelids but, at the same time, Dev's mouth on hers sprang into her mind's eye again, stoking the fire she'd been snuffing out for too long, and she felt the strangest urge to smile.

Amidst it all, she sensed Dev's presence next to her, and when Amrita's strange but soothing chant lulled to a close, Ally took a deep breath, her chest expanding with a lightness she hadn't known she had been craving. Amazing! Opening her eyes, she turned to him, expecting to share a smile, some mutual relief, but instead, she found him staring into the canopy above. His face was etched with a vulnerability she had never seen before. It shocked her.

'Are you OK?' she whispered, reaching out to brush her fingers against his arm.

Dev's gaze drifted down to meet hers, and there was a slight tremor in his voice when he spoke. 'I didn't expect…that.'

'What?' she whispered back.

He closed his eyes and drew a breath before releasing it, kneading his eyes with the heels of his hands. Ally bit back her next question. He didn't need her to question him right now. It also didn't feel quite right to admit she'd rather enjoyed the whole thing. She didn't feel so much like 'clouds before the rain' as 'sunshine after a storm', and she had Dev to thank for it. And Amrita, of course.

'You released something though, didn't you?' she said softly, unable to resist. 'Something to do with your sister.' The words slipped out of her, and she expected him to confirm it, maybe offer her a smile even if he didn't speak, but his face clouded over, as if he'd taken on the storm she'd just shifted. He sat up slowly, rubbing the back of his neck.

'We should get back to the others,' he said, without looking at her.

Ally nodded, sitting up alongside him as her heart thrummed. 'How long have we been gone?'

'Too long,' he said, as if he were speaking from a different planet all of a sudden.

What happened? she wondered as they made their way back through the trees. This time, he didn't stop to kiss her at intervals, and she followed silently behind in a cloud of his melancholy. He was probably more affected by his past than he'd admitted, and it only made her want to know him more, but he wasn't going to talk about it with her, which was fine, she reminded herself. She wasn't emotionally attached, that would never be the case here. There was no need to know *everything* about him!

Liar, the voice in her head chided.

CHAPTER EIGHT

ALLY CLUTCHED HER PHONE, shaking her head in disbelief. She was trying not to let her laughter ring too loudly through the makeshift bamboo hut that was right now serving as her personal phone booth in the back of the community centre.

'Thor, the god of thunder, is sweeping away your cobwebs already,' Ally teased, imagining her friend's face at the other end of the line.

'He's definitely not a god, and he has his issues, but, let me tell you, he has a hammer that can cause quite the storm.'

Ally snorted. Her friend was sounding like a different person already, which was so nice to hear. Also, the absurdity of their conversation about her new life in the Arctic was a welcome break from the daily rigors of the camp, and reminding people why applying mosquito repellent, herbal or otherwise, might just save their life.

'Enough about me and my polar exploits,' Larissa said now, steering the topic elsewhere. 'Tell me about your healing session.'

Ally's smirk disappeared as she was thrown right back to the other day, lying on that mat.

'Believe it or not, it felt like something shifted inside me,' she confessed, hearing how her tone turned contemplative instead of portraying the usual jokes, which were admittedly a mask Larissa had learned to see through long ago. 'I've slept like a log ever since. Maybe there is something to this whole energy work thing.'

'Ooh, mystical Ally. Never thought I'd see the day a qualified nurse says something like that.' Larissa chuckled. 'And how are things with our handsome Dr Chandran? Done the deed yet?'

'No. And it's complicated.' Ally sighed, playing with a loose thread on the curtain by the door. 'I'm thinking it might be safer to stay friends.'

'Safer? Since when did you agree to play it safe?' Larissa probed.

'Since I met a man who makes me want to wrap him up in blankets and protect him from the world,' Ally admitted. She sighed again. 'He's... vulnerable, Larissa. And I'm tired of broken things.' Ally chewed her lip; the lie felt wrong, but if she didn't put a line under it, vocally, to her friend, she might go back on her word. The thought of getting entangled with another man who was all jagged edges inside made her hesitate. Wasn't she supposed to be the reckless one here? Not the healer! He had people in the jungle for that.

'Ally, if it's no-strings, what does a bit of baggage matter? Just live in the moment for once,' Larissa urged.

'Easy for you to say; you're shacking up with a Norse deity, with issues,' she retorted. Larissa hadn't seen Dev's face that day, after the ceremony. Ally and Dev hadn't spoken about it since, but she knew whatever had happened was still on his mind. 'Anyway, baggage is baggage and he has it.' She paused. 'Just like I do.'

Just then, a shadow blocked the sun streaming through the doorway. She looked up, holding the phone away from her. It was Dev.

'Look, I gotta go,' she said to Larissa quickly. 'We'll talk later?'

'Sure thing. Stay out of trouble, and give Dev a chance to surprise you,' Larissa advised before ending the call.

'Who was that?' Dev asked as Ally pocketed the phone.

Oh, no, what did he hear?

'No one,' she said.

'Talking to yourself is the first sign of madness, you know.' He smirked.

'Or genius,' Ally shot back, recovering her composure as she turned to face him. 'I prefer to think I'm brainstorming with an expert.'

Dev nodded, and she knew he'd heard something. It was too late to pretend she hadn't been talking about him. 'Listen—' she began, but he cut her off.

'Ally, I've been meaning to talk to you.'

Uh-oh.

Dev knew he had to tell her. It had been playing on his mind ever since that ceremony. Whatever Amrita had done had brought back, not only the accident, but everything that happened after it, and, most notably, the way he'd buried himself in unsuspecting women to stop the guilt crashing back in. He was turning to Ally the closer he got to potentially going home to his family, and after what happened with Cassinda he had sworn never to hurt anyone else.

'There was someone else before—a co-worker,' he said now, and Ally crossed her arms, eyeing him with suspicion.

'OK,' she said.

'We were colleagues, as in she also worked for the NHF, and things got messy.' He might as well tell her the whole story, before she got any more ideas. 'She wanted more than I could give. She wanted me to settle down, stop moving, stop accepting assignments.' He ran a hand through his hair, picturing the way she'd blown up like a volcano in his face and started packing up her bags. 'I can't go through that again. I won't put anyone else through that…'

'Is that what you think this is?' Ally snorted. Dev looked up in surprise. 'Honestly, listen to yourself. You think I want to *trap* you?'

'No, I—' Dev faltered. This was not the reaction he'd expected. 'It's not about you,' he continued, lowering his voice as someone wheeled a cart through the community centre. They were separated by nothing but a flimsy bamboo wall. 'It's about me not wanting to hurt you—or anyone else.'

'Because you think I'm broken already,' she concluded. Behind her the colours of the sunrise were starting to paint the sky.

'No,' he said, 'but I literally just heard you say *you* were tired of broken things.'

Ally flushed and dragged her hands through her hair. 'I didn't necessarily mean that,' she countered.

'My baggage is carry-on size only, I assure you,' he quipped as she visibly squirmed. 'But I don't want to make promises I can't keep.'

Ally nodded, stepping back to put some distance between them again. She was touching her lips, feeling their future kisses disappear on the wind, probably. He did the same without thinking, mirroring her.

'I get it, Dev. Really, I do,' she said. 'And maybe

I was putting on a bit of an act for the sake of my friend, and…to protect myself. But let's be realistic. I'm leaving at the end of this. I have a home to get back to…a job!' She paused then. 'Well, I *will* find another job, but my point is, I know you're going to keep on moving. I know you don't want to settle down. I know you don't want to go home because you feel bad about how your family look at you, even though I'm sure they love you, and miss you…'

Ouch. He felt his shoulders slump for a second as her eyes widened in regret. 'I mean, oh, gosh, I'm sorry, but it's true. Isn't it?'

He shook his head, feeling the shame wash over him like an ice bath. It *was* true, and she was too observant, and too honest. And it didn't make him want her any less. He just couldn't bear the memories of Roisin everywhere at home, his family reminding him what he'd lost.

Keep on moving, keep working, keep helping other people…nothing else matters, they'll understand. Won't they?

'Anyway, Dev, I'm not looking to get hurt any more than you want to hurt me. We're both adults.' Ally stepped closer, working her jaw side to side, as if concluding something in her head. 'If we were to continue this, whatever it is, I would consider it more of an agreement.'

The tension that had knotted his shoulders

began to ease as he considered her words. She was offering him an out, a chance to maintain their connection without the weight of expectations. What happened with Cassinda couldn't happen here, basically. 'An agreement,' he repeated.

'Look,' Ally said. The determination in her eyes amused him suddenly. This woman was crazy, and he liked it. 'A fling wouldn't be the end of the world, Dev. I think we both know I'm not looking for promises. I'm not even sure if I'm ready for anything serious, maybe I never will be.' She bit her lip and diverted her gaze, as if she'd revealed a little too much.

OK, this wasn't what he'd expected either, not at all, but it *was* exactly what he needed to hear. Ally had always been straightforward, and he suspected her humour was a bit of a shield against everything she'd gone through herself, in Sicily, and back in Somerset, but now sincerity replaced sarcasm and he found himself drawn to her honesty. And the thought of more of those kisses…

Raking a hand through his hair, he searched her face for any last sign of uncertainty. He had to be sure she was being honest. His heart raced at the thought of being close to her. He'd been so damn lonely lately, and horny with all this heat, but there could be implications.

Ally crossed her arms in the other direction,

and drummed her fingers. He noticed her mosquito bites had gone down a considerable amount. 'We're adults, and we know what this is. We know what it isn't. I'm not asking for more than you can give. I've got my own baggage, remember?'

He nodded slowly, watching her perfect lips, wanting to pull them gently between his teeth. She inched closer now, and he swore he caught a flicker of doubt cross her face before she snuffed it out and looked at him from under her eyelashes. 'Just don't fall for me, Doctor,' she said.

His body responded to her proximity before his mind could keep up. Dev pressed his mouth to hers, claiming her lips as if he had no other choice. Her magnetism was always going to win over his resolve. She moaned against his mouth, ramming her hands in his hair again, then down his back, digging her nails in, leaving her mark.

'OK, then,' he breathed, training a thumb over her bottom lip. 'Let's keep it simple.'

'Simple,' she echoed with a slight quirk of her lips. He couldn't fight the smile. A promise wrapped in a single word. An invitation. Without thinking any more, he swept a hand behind her head and closed the gap again. The kiss grew hotter and hotter and only when her hands began unbuttoning his shirt did he remember where they were. The community centre was bustling outside and she stifled a laugh, forcing herself backwards, smoothing down her hair.

'You're going to ruin me,' he growled, doing his shirt back up with a groan. Ally was watching him, lips swollen, eyes narrowed.

'Rule number one: No falling in love,' she said.

'Ha! As if,' he scoffed, his laughter a little too sharp. He caught the flicker of something in Ally's expression, the same vulnerability he'd seen when he'd learned how she and her sister had blamed themselves for what had happened, until deciding it was no one's fault. Different from what happened with Roisin, he thought, as a flash of darkness cast a fresh shadow on their conversation. That had been his fault, even if no one else had ever let him believe it.

Was this a good idea? What if she developed feelings and tried to pin him down, as Cassinda had, even after promising not to? Being in one place was dangerous—that was when you started letting people in, developing ties and emotions.

'Rule number two: We stop if it stops being fun,' she proposed next, her voice dropping to a more serious note.

'Fun,' he echoed, tasting the word. It sounded simple enough, yet the weight of a million potential complications bore down on him like baby elephants. They hadn't even slept together yet but this chemistry was crazy. It could keep him still, focused on her. The danger zone. It could put a real dent in his professional integrity, too.

'Or we could just stick to being plague-fighting buddies,' she added, lifting an eyebrow in a playful challenge.

'Plague-fighting buddies?' he repeated, unable to suppress a snort. 'Sounds like a bad comic-book duo.'

'Bad or brilliant?' Ally's grin was infectious, and Dev found his face stretching into a cat-like smile despite the tumult that was starting to feel a lot like a collective of crickets bouncing about in his abdomen. Some of the tension had lifted, at least. Before he could reply, she stepped towards him boldly and claimed the back of his neck with both hands.

Dev's hands roamed down her back and he couldn't help but feel a thrill at the way she all but melted into his arms, time and time again, as if she belonged there. It had been so long since he'd allowed himself to feel desired, wanted by someone who knew exactly how to touch him and make him feel like this…as if he was finally getting out of his own head.

Just as things started to get heated again, Dev pulled back abruptly, leaving Ally breathless. He'd been somewhere else entirely but he'd come here with another purpose.

'I actually came to tell you something else,' he

said now, and, reluctantly, she released his crinkled shirt from her grip. 'We've all been invited to dinner,' he told her in a low voice, right into her ear. 'Time to act like we don't want to tear each other's clothes off.'

'Plenty of time for that later,' she responded, and it was all he could do to calm the bulge in his pants long enough to make an exit.

Ally's gaze wandered beyond the clinking glasses and animated faces, and rested on the lush tapestry of green cascading with the waterfall down the rolling hill. The elevated terrace where the NHF team had gathered for a special dinner to honour their last night on the malaria project was buzzing with the kind of warmth their Kerala hosts had quickly become known for throughout their posting. Their group were being treated to an array of local foods by the villagers, who were grateful for their work over the last week and were sorry to be seeing them go tomorrow, and Ally breathed it all in as she dug a fork into a chunk of spicy broccoli, feeling happy. Yes, that was it. She was happy. Content. It felt nice to be happy and content for once.

'I could get used to dinners like this.' Dev's voice brought her back to herself, his dark eyes reflecting the myriad lights. Dusk was settling over the landscape now and a soft glow from overhead lanterns dappled over the tables, casting an extra vibe of enchantment over the scene. 'Better than rice and peas.'

'Much—why is it always rice and peas lately?' she replied, her heart skipping a beat as memories of their last kiss sent a thrill down her spine. Tucking a stray strand of hair behind her ear, she lowered her voice. 'Maybe the food will be better when we move on tomorrow, to the maternal health camp. And maybe you won't ignore me there.'

'I have to ignore you. Because if I don't, I will kiss you in front of all these people,' he replied in a growl, trailing a hand over her knee with delicate fingers under the table. She suppressed a groan as it inched part way up her thigh, before she coughed and crossed her legs, essentially shooing him away. He was telling the truth. They'd been avoiding talking to each other since sitting down, even though they had purposely sat next to each other and the magnets were still doing their thing.

'Make it up to me later,' she told him. 'I dare you.' *Where is this confidence coming from?*

'That won't be a problem. In fact, let's seal that promise,' he said, raising his glass in a mock toast. Without even knowing what they were toasting, everyone at the table raised their glasses.

'To us,' Ally said, clinking a round of glasses.

She couldn't help but laugh, but uh-oh. Was this being entirely unprofessional, and silly? she thought as laughter rippled between them, along with a fresh tangle of excitement and trepidation. Yes, it probably was silly. She'd entered that conversation with a certain amount of bravado in the heat of the moment, and even told him they should stop if it stopped being fun, but she already knew she was incapable of *not* developing feelings for a guy she was kissing at every occasion. His guilt over that ex-colleague, and his sister, coupled with her own propensity to unleash a maelstrom of emotion at any moment meant they shared a heavy load, but she just needed to keep reminding herself to be who he thought she was: fun, a functioning adult, perfectly capable of a meaningless fling.

'Stay out of your own head,' she muttered.

Dev smiled, as if to say, *Caught you talking to yourself again, weirdo.*

He started talking to someone else at the table, and Ally found herself in a conversation with their medical assistant, Aryan. Soon their chat was interrupted by a loud laugh that sounded far too smug for her liking. Ally turned her attention momentarily to the left, where Dev was still talking to another colleague, who might or might not have had too many beers. But that wasn't what held her attention. Dev's words floated over to her, clear and immediately jarring: 'Honestly, I'm single by choice. I can't imagine *anything* tying me down. I enjoy travelling too much.'

'Yeah, I'm the same, mate,' the guy agreed, clinking his beer can to Dev's glass of water.

A pang of annoyance pricked at Ally as she reached for her own drink, feeling her smile and happy buzz both faltering for a moment. It wasn't as though she expected declarations of love, far from it, but hearing Dev's cavalier dismissal of attachments literally hours after their last intimate encounter stung more than she cared to admit, especially after he'd so enthusiastically agreed on their...well...agreement. Was this for her benefit? She shot him a look of annoyance down her nose, but if he registered it, he didn't react.

'Man, that's the spirit,' one of the other doctors lauded now, clapping Dev on the back. 'Freedom to roam the world—that's living the dream.'

'Definitely,' a female volunteer chimed in, her admiration thinly veiled as she glanced Dev's way through her eyelashes.

Ally noted the mixed reactions—surprise flickering across some faces, nods of respect from others. She forced a laugh, aligning herself with the majority, while, inside, a quiet resolve took a stranglehold on her heart. If Dev's world had no room for anchors, she'd be wise to remember to ride the waves, so to speak, not sink beneath them. If Dev could enjoy these stolen moments for the fun they were, without looking back, so could she. In fact, she would initiate them. Lots of them. That was one way to stay in control, she reasoned.

But it wasn't just that bugging her, she realised later, when people were packing up for the night and she was smearing more of her magic anti-mosquito potion all over her legs. Dev was running away from things he needed to face, things with his family, if what he'd said was anything to go by. They missed him, surely, and, romances aside, he was doing all this 'travelling' in order to stay away from them, out of guilt for something he hadn't done. How infuriating that she was starting to know the real him, when everyone else saw only what he thought they wanted to see. But was it really her place to bring it up again?

As Ally and Dev made their way down the winding path back towards the guest house, the rumbles in the distance crept closer, until they were right above their heads.

'I think it's going to—' she started just as the sky opened up, releasing a torrent of heavy rain that felt as though someone in the treetops had upended a barrel of water over them, a proper downfall, not one of those bouts of measly drizzle she often encountered back home. This was real rain with a purpose. They ran, laughing as the downpour soaked through their clothes. Ally's dress was growing more transparent by the minute.

'Come on! You're too slow,' Dev called, grabbing her hand.

'You're taller than me—with those legs you're a gazelle compared to me!'

'Are you comparing me to a beast?' He laughed, pulling her into the shelter of a large banyan tree as the rain lashed at the ground all around them. His eyes sparkled with mischief, right before he kissed her. For a heartbeat, she sank completely into him, feeling his hands caressing her face, then her backside. His words at the dinner table charged back into her head, but what was the point of caring now?

He urged her closer with intent and deepened their kiss, his tongue dancing with hers as his hands roamed up her back to her hair, tugging gently on the strands, then harder. It was so erotic she could hardly stand it. He pushed himself deeper against her, and Ally let out another soft moan, her body melting into his as she responded to his touch by wrapping a leg around his middle. She could feel the rainwater dripping down her neck and back, her skin tingling from the sudden cold mixed with a thousand new sensations all hitting her at once. She'd never been this turned on, ever.

Their lips parted and they gasped for air before another kiss plunged them deeper into this entirely new world where she could not have stopped if she tried. His back was against the tree, her hips crushed to his. In an instant, the playful banter had shifted into something charged, something electric. Their laughter subsided into heavy breaths as they stood there kissing, the rain cascading around them with force. Ally could feel the desire emanating from his body mounting as his lips crashed against hers hungrily, and his hands hoisted the fabric of her wet dress up. She wrapped her arms around his neck and pulled him closer.

His lips worked like magic, sending shivers down her spine and making her dizzy with want. She pushed herself against him harder, arching her back to feel his hips pressed harder against hers.

The scent of wet earth swept her up with his cologne as they kissed desperately, hungrily, as if there were no tomorrow, and the world seemed to narrow down to the very space they occupied, to the sensation of his hands on her skin, the hardness of him pressed to her thigh.

'We should probably get out of these wet clothes before we both catch pneumonia,' he said against her lips. Somehow, even the word *pneumonia* sounded too sexy for her to resist pressing her mouth back to his again.

'Stay with me tonight,' Ally whispered, her fingers tracing the line of his jaw as she found her breath. She was panting, dizzy, and the words slipped out, so bold! Where was this raw desire coming from all of a sudden? A fight for control…because he wouldn't be sticking around?

Don't think about that!

All she cared about as he held her close was seizing this moment and exploring this connection before it slipped away. It was definitely going to slip away. He'd made that clear. And she was fine with it.

They dashed the remaining distance to the guest house.

CHAPTER NINE

ALLY'S BEDROOM DOOR clicked shut behind them, her shushes filling the space as Dev stumbled with her into the dimly lit room. The rain had completely soaked through their clothes, even more during the mad dash back to the guest house, and now, in Ally's warm room, in the dark and quiet, the reality of their entwined figures was setting every one of his nerve endings on fire. Whatever this was, it was too late to stop now, and it didn't seem as though either of them wanted to either.

Their mutual urgency was almost comical, hands grappling at damp fabric, tearing away every layer that separated skin from skin. The thud of wet clothes hitting the floor shot through the silence, and he held her naked frame to his chest from behind, letting his fingers trace the contours of her back, following the water droplets sliding over her shoulders. In truth he was trying to memorise the path of every curve without her clothes concealing her body, and she was perfect. So perfect, in fact, he was increasingly glad he'd made that announcement at the dinner table, about nothing tying him down.

His thoughts betrayed him as he turned her around and kissed her, flickering back to the phone call he'd overheard. 'He's…vulnerable, Larissa. And I'm tired of broken things.' She'd said it, and he'd heard it, taken it through to his core. He had vocally feigned indifference about relationships to keep her from seeing just how much her words had affected him once the thrill of their stolen kisses and the agreement had subsided slightly. How could he reveal the depth of his growing affection when she was right, he was carrying baggage, more than she deserved to try and carry along with him? Yet somehow he could not keep away.

'Dev,' she breathed out, pulling him onto the bed with her, and wrapping her legs around him. He'd been lost in the sensation of her kisses, and her fingers tangling in his wet hair. 'I want you.'

'Are you sure?'

'Do I look unsure?' she replied with a breathless laugh, tightening the grip of her thighs around his middle. Her eyes reflected a hunger that definitely matched his own, even though he was acutely aware of the vulnerability behind his facade. He should be anywhere but here, in Ally's bedroom, with her skin all radiant and flushed, and their rain-soaked clothes discarded all over the floor, but from the intensity that crackled between them like a live wire she was determined to live out this agreement and he wasn't going to retract everything he'd said either. They were adults, they knew their boundaries.

She reached for the foil packet on the nightstand, which he noticed she'd taken out of the drawer discreetly while they'd been making out. He searched her face for any sign of hesitation, any trace of doubt. He found none—only an affirmation that what they were doing felt right despite all the reasons it shouldn't.

'Promise me something?' Ally asked, drawing him closer.

'I thought you weren't looking for promises,' he replied. His heart thumped with anticipation and something else he couldn't quite name as he hovered above Ally.

'Let's just…let's just be here, now. No past, no future. Just us.'

She said it as if she was trying to convince herself of something. 'OK,' was all he could seem to say in response. For a moment, he allowed himself the luxury of being present, of feeling her beneath him, around him, a connection he hadn't expected to make.

'You love making deals, don't you?' he teased, running his hands along the smooth skin of her arms.

'I do.' She smiled, and her gaze said she wanted him more than her roving hands did.

Then, the shrill ring of her phone sliced through the thick air of the bedroom like a scalpel. He watched her eyes widen as she scrambled naked from beneath him to grab the device from the nightstand.

'Hello?' Her voice was breathless, and definitely carried more than a hint of what they'd just been about to do. He pulled the sheet around him and lay on his back, staring at the ceiling fan, catching his breath. The room was so quiet he could hear the voice on the other end of the line, even without her putting it on speakerphone.

'Ally? It's Nora. I need you; it's about Oliver...' The female voice was strained, edged with urgency, and Dev could feel the shift in the atmosphere, as if the temperature had suddenly dropped.

'Is he OK?' The concern in Ally's tone was palpable, and Dev found himself holding his breath, silently willing everything to be all right. It must be her sister. He recalled the name, Nora, and Oliver too. Her nephew.

'He's... It's just been a tough day, and he's asking for you. Can you talk to him?'

'Of course, put him on.' Ally glanced apologetically at Dev. Her eyes were clouded with worry. He nodded, mimed that she shouldn't worry about him.

'Hey, sweetie, what's up?' The transition from the passionate lover Ally had almost been just now to caring aunt was seamless, and Dev felt a twinge of something that might have been envy. She made it seem so easy. Should he go? He felt like a spare part suddenly, as if they'd physically entered the room and caught him naked.

'Can you read my story, Aunt Ally? I worked really hard on it,' came the small, hopeful voice that Dev assumed was Oliver's.

'Send it over, Ollie. I'll read it right now…oh, you want me to listen? Um…sure, I'd love to.'

She put her hand over the phone for a second. Sorry, she mouthed to him, already moving to sit at the small desk by the window, her wet clothes forgotten on the floor as she pulled a robe around her body.

'Take your time,' Dev replied, the words feeling hollow as he pushed himself off the bed. He grabbed a towel and wrapped it around his waist. An odd sense of displacement settled over him as he watched her switch gears so effortlessly.

He retrieved a glass of water from the bathroom, returning to find Ally absorbed in her nephew's story. The affectionate smile playing on her lips as she listened softened something inside him. It reminded him why he'd been drawn to her in the first place: she was fun and hardworking and kind... This nurturing spirit he was seeing now was so damn attractive in a woman. For a second, he could imagine her tucking a kid into bed, reading a story. For another second that surprised him he imagined himself bringing her a cup of tea while she was doing it, perching on the end of the bed.

'Listen to this bit, Dev,' Ally said, putting a hand over the receiver again as he sat down tentatively. 'And then the brave alien defender decided that no intergalactic monster was too big to fight if it meant protecting his family.' She repeated her nephew's words and laughed softly, and he could hear she was bursting with pride. 'He's got quite the imagination, our little Ollie. And such a good heart.'

'Sounds like someone else I know,' he mused, his thoughts drifting involuntarily to the email from his brother that he'd been dodging. The contrast between Ally's fierce loyalty to her family and his own strained ties didn't exactly make him feel all that great right now. In fact, all this was leaving him feeling exposed, as if she were unwittingly holding up a mirror, reflecting all his inadequacies. He cleared his throat, started gathering up his clothes from the floor, and she watched him, frowning down her nose.

'Just come back in ten minutes?' she said, holding her hand over the phone.

'I'm pretty tired,' he murmured, leaning in to drop a soft kiss to her forehead. She pulled away, shot him a look of surprise that might have been tinged with hurt, but he knew he'd killed the passion now, and he wasn't about to fake that it would just come back in ten minutes. Slowly, he crept out of the room with his clothes, and shut the door behind him.

Dev adjusted the straps of the medical supply bags slung over his shoulder as he took in the maternal health camp that the team had set up. The air was alive with a melting pot of languages. Healthcare professionals carried things between tents, while expectant mothers clustered in groups, some with wide-eyed children clinging to their colourful skirts.

The goal at this specific, and already far too humid, location was to help minimise complications and ensure a safe birthing environment for the women who would otherwise not have access to such care. But, as with all assignments, no one knew what kind of situations they might be asked to deal with in yet another small village tucked away between mountains and jungle.

And this thing with Ally was already another 'situation' Dev wasn't sure how to handle. Where did they stand after last night? She'd left the guest house early this morning and made her way here on another truck, without him. Tonight, they would all move as a group to new lodgings. Tents. Already he was dreading it; he never slept well in tents, and it was even harder to find any privacy on campsites.

At least he'd have another excuse for not having Wi-Fi, he thought before he could stop it. No...he would reply to his mother. And he would consider going home for Roisin's birthday. Ally had made him think, and truly take to heart what a terrible son and brother he was being. It stung more after last night.

'Over here,' she directed now, her voice cutting through the hum of conversations. Ally was standing ten feet across the site in her shorts and a shirt, her white coat loose over the top, and her red hair shining in the sun, piled high on the top of her head. Boxes of medical supplies bulged open by the table she was setting up under a canvas canopy, and the water dispenser was already half empty, as usual. The heat was more intense than ever today, and already Dev could feel the sweat clinging to his neck under his collar. Together, they began to unpack, setting up their workstations beside each other without discussing it.

'How are you this morning?' she asked a little frostily, without looking at him.

'Good. Ally, can we talk?' he asked after a moment.

She didn't meet his gaze and focused instead on adjusting the nearby incubator's settings. 'Not now, Dev.'

'Later, then.' His voice was steadier than he felt, but he respected her evasion. The underlying current of defensiveness in her tone was obvious.

'Later,' she agreed, though the word hung in the air like a placeholder for a conversation he knew she didn't particularly want to have.

He soon found himself seeing to a young expectant mother with a standard check-up, and a little nutritional advice; it wasn't doing her much good, only eating vegetables in accordance with her religious beliefs. She ran the risk of becoming anaemic.

He felt Ally's eyes on him as a five-year-old girl wandered over, clutching her doll. Dev hunkered down to her level with a warm smile. She introduced the doll as her baby sister, a role-play they encouraged in these camps to educate older siblings about newborn care. Soon he was showing the girl how to support the doll's head, and his gaze flitted once again to Ally. She was cradling an infant in one arm, feeding him from a small bottle filled with formula. Right until the bottle seemed to crack and milk started spilling everywhere.

'Need a hand with that?' he asked, making his way to her side as she put the child down gently and struggled with a stubborn box of new bottles. They were here to provide essential medical care to expectant mothers and new mothers alike, and as such the team was prepared to offer all manner of prenatal care, postnatal check-ups and even childbirth if it came to it. But whoever he found himself talking to, his mind lagged behind, and his eyes wandered to Ally, replaying what had happened the night before. She was obviously still annoyed with him for just leaving.

'Got it, thanks,' she said, tearing the tape off a bit too quickly and almost causing the box to topple over.

He caught it deftly, and she smiled and muttered thanks, but it didn't quite reach her eyes. In minutes he was called away to attend to another patient, which he was glad about, considering her coldness was giving him frostbite despite it being a thousand degrees out. If only he could keep his mind from drifting back to her naked body exposed beneath him. They'd been so close. They would have kept that hook-up going all night, got zero sleep. Maybe it was better they'd been interrupted, he mused, swiping at his forehead. He was already feeling things he wasn't sure what to do with around her. Even her rejection just now grated at him in ways it shouldn't; usually he'd put his emotions completely aside and focus on the job.

Their silent dance of awkward coordination and stolen looks was disrupted when a local volunteer approached, calling for help. Straight away Dev abandoned his station again and crossed to where the guy was cradling a small form wrapped in a threadbare blanket. Dev's heart plummeted.

'Doctor,' the man called out again, his voice laced with urgency. 'They must have known you were coming. They just left him here in the bushes! Can you look?'

Sensing the commotion, Ally's snapped her head up, and she crossed the distance in seconds. Dev watched as she gently took the baby into her arms before he could, uncovering the tiny, yellow-tinged face of the jaundiced infant. The baby's skin was pale and his body frail, and Dev's heart squeezed at the sight of it, the vulnerability...the look on Ally's face as she held it close.

'Malnourished, by the look of it, and abandoned,' he heard himself say, brushing Ally's fingers as they both went to touch the child. 'Tough start to life.'

'Let's run a check,' Ally murmured at him,

already moving towards the incubator with the baby cradled close. She was handling the tot so carefully and calmly, but Dev could see the dogged determination in her face as Ally checked the baby's pulse, her fingers pressing delicately against the tiny wrist. His own hands moved seemingly of their own accord, prepping needles and drawing fluids for intravenous hydration.

'Likely hypoglycaemic,' he said quietly, focusing on measuring out a precise dose of dextrose. His gaze flickered to Ally as he handed her the syringe, her usually lively blue eyes clouded with concern. She took it from him with a nod, her hand steady as she found a vein and administered the solution. The baby cried out again and she shushed it, not leaving his side, even as Dev slipped off to see to a few other patients.

'All right, Sahil,' she whispered to the baby, when Dev returned to her side after several long minutes seeing to yet another pregnant teenager. They really needed to have a talk about contraception around here.

'Sahil?' He cocked an eyebrow.

'I named him. I had to,' she explained, and he watched the baby's tiny fingers curl around one of hers. Maybe it was a mistake to name him, he thought. Didn't that mean she'd grow attached? They should both know enough about the dangers of that by now, but how could he say that? Thankfully the baby seemed to have calmed down just a little under Ally's careful touch and attention. 'We need to get him on some nutritional supplements,' she told him, and this time she looked up, catching his eyes.

'He'll be OK,' he told her, needing to say something to reassure her. For now, they were a team. And having seen how maternal she was, at least with her nephew, Oliver, he knew it was important to her that they both do everything in their power to help this child... Sahil...get a better start than just being abandoned in a bush for anyone to discover.

Dev fetched the necessary equipment from the tent nearby. He returned with a small bottle filled with liquid vitamins and minerals prescribed for malnutrition cases like this one, and watched as Ally tried to feed the child. The baby seemed hesitant at first but eventually started suckling on it, his little body trembling with each gulp. Dev felt his heart expand and contract as her eyes reflected an ocean of compassion, the same look that always shifted something inside him. She extended her attention so effortlessly from her family to even the smallest, most forgotten lives, like this one. Her nurturing nature contrasted so sharply with the walls he'd built around his own heart, he might as well be wearing knives, and he'd barely even noticed how it had affected everything around him, till now.

His thoughts were interrupted by Sahil's soft cries. His tiny fists were clinging onto Ally's loose coat now, as if he were aware of their efforts to save him and was begging not to be abandoned again.

'We won't let any more harm come to you, sweet one,' Ally whispered, and Dev hoped they would be able to ensure that actually happened. 'We will, won't we?' she asked him now, quietly. There was so much hope in her eyes he couldn't stand it. If local organisations couldn't locate the child's birth mother, abandoned babies were often placed in orphanages or children's homes operated by the government or NGOs. He told her this, and she nodded thoughtfully. 'In some cases, babies like this are placed in foster care with temporary caregivers.'

'I know some people feel like they don't have a choice but to give up their child,' she said, brushing a thumb across the baby's soft cheek as he looked over her shoulder. 'I mean, how do you know what you'd do in any situation, if you came from a broken home, or you were too poor to care for it, I suppose…but I just… I couldn't.'

Dev stopped himself from putting a supportive hand on her shoulder. There didn't seem to be any words. He could tell by the look on her face how heartbreaking she was finding this, but in truth it wasn't the first abandoned baby he had seen across his missions with the NHF. Only now he was able to look at it through the lens of a woman he cared about, a woman who clearly had strong maternal instincts.

His own mother, who'd been nothing short of doting to her kids, growing up, must spend an awful lot of time wondering where he was... out here, flitting about, largely uncontactable, avoiding home because of the memories they themselves lived with every single day, in the very same house. Not for the first time, he saw his unforgivable distance through her eyes, and he didn't like himself very much for adding to his mother's trauma when she'd already lost one child.

'Excuse me,' he said to Ally now. 'I really have to go and make a call.'

CHAPTER TEN

ALLY'S BOOTS CRUNCHED on the underbrush as she and Dev trailed behind the chattering gaggle of local children, their chirpy voices weaving through the dense forest like sunlight between leaves. It was hot, as usual, and Ally was tired, what with the drama of doing everything in her power to ensure that poor baby Sahil was OK. He was doing much better than yesterday when they'd found him, thankfully, and he was now resting in the care of their local volunteers, but she was worried about his fate. There were so many children and worried parents and expectant mothers to see on this assignment. It was the most stressful one yet.

There was Dev, too, she thought, glancing back to find him trailing her, probably looking out for leopards and snakes and whatever else was waiting to eat her now that the mosquitos had finally grown tired of her taste. Dev's hot mouth and lingering kisses and eyes that could undo her were another reason for her skyrocketing stress levels and sleepless night last night. She'd lain awake, thinking about Oliver, and the fact that Dev had sneaked out of her room after they'd been about to do the deed. Charming! After today, all she wanted to do was head to their next campsite, locate her tent, and sleep. But these kids had seemed bursting with excitement to share something with their visitors from afar, and she couldn't exactly say no.

'*Anayude kulikkam kandu!*' one boy shouted over his shoulder now, wriggling his finger eagerly ahead.

Dev ambled up beside them, his tall, broad frame looking ridiculously good today in a T-shirt the colour of the leaves. 'They're excited for you to see the elephants bathing,' he explained, brushing a branch aside before she could walk into it. 'It's a tradition here.'

'Thank you, Dev,' Ally said, a little too coldly in light of all this wonderment around her. She had always been better than average at masking her feelings with humour, in fact, she was a pro at it, but in this moment, there was no need for a facade. He knew she was annoyed. That was why he'd tried to talk to her earlier. But the stubborn part of her was not going to let him off. He was scowling now, to himself, and she let out a frustrated sigh.

'Well, you just disappeared,' she said, keeping her voice low. 'I thought we were going to—'

'We *were* going to,' he finished, coming up beside her properly, making her nerve-endings fizz with the instant proximity. 'I'm sorry, OK, you just seemed busy.'

'Was that all it was?' she asked him. 'It seemed like I did something to scare you off.'

Dev went to reply, but stopped himself, chewing down on his lip, and she sighed again, pushing forward, forcing her shoulders to stay squared even as a palm branch swiped her round the face. If he wasn't going to talk to her, she wasn't going to force him. Maybe that agreement had been a stupid idea anyway. It was already more trouble than it was worth.

As they drew closer to the spring, the air grew even thicker with the symphony of nature's sounds. Ally was starting to recognise the calls of different exotic birds and enjoy the carefree laughter of the children at play. They seemed to live with the kind of simplicity that kids back home could probably never imagine. She couldn't help but be swept up in the infectious joy of it all, and soon she found herself forgetting her annoyance and fatigue and joining in their games, though she could feel Dev's eyes on her hair flying behind her as she chased the little ones through the jungle paths, laughing and ducking under low-hanging branches.

'Tag! You're it!' she called out, tapping a giggling girl on the back before darting away, pretending to trumpet like an elephant. The child squealed with delight and gave chase, her bare feet kicking up dirt as she followed the sun-speckled path. The heat clung to Ally like a second skin, sweat beading along her forehead. As she dodged behind what looked like a cabin in the undergrowth, shaded and almost hidden by vines, to evade her pursuer, a brief respite allowed her the space to breathe. But Dev rounded the corner in a flash and stopped right in front of her.

The feel of his kisses lodged in her mind, stubborn and intrusive as she ran her eyes over his, then down to his mouth. 'I see you found the kids' secret hideout,' he said, stepping closer, till he was obstructing her entire vision.

She pressed her back to the corrugated wall. 'What is this place?'

'It used to be a hunter's lodge,' he said, and she drew a breath, remembering the look on his face, how he had left her room so abruptly just as things were getting intimate.

'Does that make me your prey?' she whispered.

All she could think of was the warmth of skin on skin that had felt like nothing else she'd ever experienced, even with Matt. But as a result of those feelings, all swirling dangerously inside her, he'd also left her feeling rejected when he'd left last night, and hadn't even thought to come back as she'd asked.

'I'm sorry,' he said again, cupping her face. She leaned into his palm and closed her eyes, wishing she could stay angry. 'It wasn't that you did something to scare me off. Me leaving was not a reflection on you.'

Ally felt her jaw twitch. 'So what was it?' Why wouldn't he just talk to her?

'Ally, come on!' A small boy had run back for her, and was tugging at her hand, bringing her back to the present. She pulled herself away from the vine-covered wall, motioning for Dev to come, too. The laughter of the children up ahead by the spring mingled with the distant trumpet of an elephant and the sound felt like both a warning and a welcome.

Ally found a secluded, shady spot by the spring. There were four elephants here already.

'Are they dangerous?' Ally asked, her gaze following the gentle giants as they rolled and splashed in the late afternoon sun. Their hides, rough and weathered, glistened under the warm rays.

'Usually only if they're provoked,' Dev replied, sitting next to her as the children scattered along the water's edge, keeping a safe distance. Some produced sketchbooks and pencils. 'But it's best to respect their space.'

As the elephants bathed, there was a simplicity in their movements, a ritualistic grace that soothed Ally's restless thoughts. She let out a breath and allowed herself a moment just to be— to watch these animals, so ancient and wise, reclaiming something she supposed had been lost in human nature. How often did she just sit, and think, and be? It was tough to do that, what with all the thoughts that rushed back in every time she forgot to block them out.

Ally turned towards Dev, his profile cut against the backdrop of the forest. 'I'm sorry too, for being distant today,' she started, the words clumsy in her mouth. 'When you left last night... I guess I felt a little rejected. I haven't done... this...' she wiggled a finger between them both '...in a pretty long time. I know I always rush to talk to them whenever they call. It's a sense of duty, I suppose.'

Dev's expression was unreadable for a moment before he nodded slowly, understanding dawning in his brown eyes. 'That sense of duty is one of the things I admire about you,' he said. 'But it does make me reflect on how bad of a son, and brother, I am. That's why I left last night.' He brushed her shoulder on purpose with his, and goosebumps shot down her arm.

Ally bit her lip, considering. 'OK.'

'I've been avoiding giving my family an answer about my sister's birthday event.'

'Valentine's Day, right?'

'Yes. But I've told them I'll go now. Told them this morning.'

'Really?' Ally looked to him in surprise. She'd seen him on his phone today, with a look of consternation on his face. But if he was planning to return to Canada for Valentine's Day, it meant he'd be leaving in two weeks, or less, and before her. 'I mean, that's great, of course you should go home,' she said, doing her best not to sound concerned. 'Will you be back, afterwards?'

She watched a smile tug at his lips, and she realised she had sounded more hopeful about that than she'd intended. Dev just shrugged as she pulled her eyes away. 'Maybe, but usually if you leave an assignment early, you're just assigned a new one wherever they need you next. Especially as this one's so far from Canada.'

Ally felt his hand on hers, and the subtle gesture went some way to curbing the wild fluttering in her stomach. He could be gone so soon, and she'd probably never see this man again. 'Ally,' he said softly. The intimacy of the contact and the tone of his voice drew her gaze from the children's games to his face again. His eyes were pools of questions. He opened his mouth to speak, but she cut him off.

'Well, I guess that's it for us. Our agreement,' she said quickly, as rejection settled right back into the place he'd just removed it from. It wasn't fair, or right, to feel this way, but she couldn't help it.

'Neither of us entered into this thinking it would last,' he reminded her gently, running a thumb along the back of her hand. Ally's mind swam, even as she let her head fall softly against his shoulder.

'I know,' she said. 'It's just not easy for me, letting people in. Not any more,' she admitted. 'And I did it with you anyway, for some reason. Stupid of me, really.'

'Not stupid,' Dev said, and she could feel him choosing his words carefully. 'After what you've been through, I get why this whole thing was harder for you to initiate than you're making out. I do, Ally, don't think I don't see that.'

Ally felt her pulse throb. She drew her knees up to her chest, wrapping an arm around them. He could obviously tell she was watching their time together come to an end before it even had, because he exhaled long and hard. 'This is… We should just stop,' he said resolutely, though he didn't let go of her hand.

'We *should* stop,' she agreed, but the silence

stretched on and she didn't let go of his hand either.

An elephant trumpeted, making the kids shriek, and Dev gave a flutter of a laugh that shook her head, making her lean into him more. Her other hand felt for his shirt, balling it in her fingers, drawing him closer still.

I'm scared, Ally wanted to confess suddenly. I am scared of stopping, and also of not stopping. I am scared of falling in love and then losing it all, all over again. Her other hand twitched beneath his, betraying the turmoil that was making a total mess of her insides. She couldn't say it, she couldn't even admit it to herself, that she was falling for a man she barely knew, a man she hadn't even slept with yet. And that she was going to miss him madly. She had promised herself, and him, that this wouldn't happen!

Dev's thumb was still drawing small circles on the back of her hand in a calming rhythm that anchored her to the moment. He looked away for a second, as if gathering his thoughts, before turning back to her.

'I don't want to complicate your life, Ally,' he began, his voice carrying a tremor she had never heard before.

'I know.'

He shook his head, squinting into the sun. 'After the car accident, everything changed. My relationship with Mom was pretty strained. She was always reaching out, and I gave her barely anything back. I think in some way I've been waiting for her to get mad, so she could direct her anger at me like I deserve. And dreading it, too.'

'You don't deserve anyone's anger, Dev,' she reminded him. 'And I bet no one is angry at you!'

He just set his mouth into a line, shook his head. 'I owe it to her to be the son she feels like she's lost,' he said. 'I need to be there for my family more, like you're there for yours.'

The silence stretched on. Ally drew a breath.

'So what happened, the night of the accident?' she asked softly, the word *accident* hanging in the air between them for what felt like an eternity. Dev stared at the elephants but kept the circles going on the back of her hand, as if she was grounding him.

'I took a different road that night. A shortcut. Roisin was drunk, distracting me...'

Ally listened, her heart aching at the raw honesty in his voice as he told her about the driver in the other car coming too fast in the other direction, how he tried to swerve but left it just a second too late. She pictured him, young and carefree, a life altered in an instant by a twist of fate. No one was immune to tragedy. The lump in her throat felt like a football, and she hesitated before voicing the question that had been nagging at her. 'But you want to keep on travelling, whatever happens with your family?'

Dev's gaze returned to hers, steadfast. 'Of course. There are still so many people out there who need help, and I can't imagine not being part of that. Working with NHF...it's part of who I am.'

'Even if it means leaving things—or people— behind?' she asked, a hint of uncertainty lacing her words.

'Even then,' he said, yet his fingers tightened around hers, suggesting he wasn't ready to sever this connection just yet. Then he looked at her sideways as if an idea was brewing in his head. 'What about you? Has this given you a taste for something else, a life on the move?'

Ally shook her head slowly, weighing it up. The thought of not returning to her sister, to the life she'd put on hold, didn't sit right and she felt it right through to her bones. Living the kind of life Dev lived wasn't an option for her. She had Nora and Oliver to think of. They needed her. And Larissa. Larissa was her best friend, and she needed her too. She was needed at home. And home was *home*, it always had been, even if she loved it here, even if she felt needed and use-ful in a way she hadn't at the clinic, amongst all these people who had no clue what it was like to have the facilities they enjoyed in other parts of the world but were, for the most part, happy and grateful and full of life!

Dev was looking at her intently, and she knew he was reading her mind. They were doomed. This agreement was already in ashes. They sat in silence for a moment, each lost in contemplation. Then, as if drawn by an invisible string, they turned their attention back to each other and, in seconds, Dev was kissing her again. Slowly at first, as if he were saying goodbye, but hidden from the children, in the shade of the trees, she was soon on her back, her legs wrapped around his middle, and he was hovering over her as though they were back in the bedroom, picking up where they'd left off.

She gasped as he started running his mouth along her lips and neck and chest in earnest, moaning her name, clutching her hand above her head as she reached for him with the other. She responded to every move hungrily, surprised at how her body was reacting to this cocktail of passion and torture. In the background she could hear the children playing by the spring, their laughter mingling with the sound of water splashing against rocks, the elephants, but they couldn't seem to let each other go.

'Come on,' Dev said suddenly, standing up and pulling her to her feet. 'Let's join them. I'm getting too hot.'

Ally looked up, breathless, smoothing herself down. She couldn't even find the words. What was happening? Weren't they stopping…this?

Still, she laughed as she felt the cool water splash against her legs, her hand still firmly grasped in Dev's, the kids jumping and splashing around them, a safe distance from the elephants, who didn't look bothered by anything at all. The playfulness of the moment was infectious, and she gave herself permission to forget about the future, or whatever else she might lose. Doomed or not, maybe it was time she and Dev both learnt to live every day as if it could be their last, and not think about the fact that all this was leading nowhere fast.

CHAPTER ELEVEN

DEV ZIPPED THE tent flap closed, sealing away the wind that was kicking up outside in the cool early dawn. The space, lit by a single overhead lamp, seemed to shrink as he turned to face Ally. She was sitting cross-legged on her sleeping bag, and her face told him exactly how she was feeling, as usual.

'Hard to believe Sahil is gone,' he murmured, his voice low and heavy with the same emotion he saw etched into her pout. Why hide it, at this point? They'd shared everything this past week at the maternity camp, and not just their skill sets. He perched on the edge of her bed. The weight and intensity of their shared experiences here had been drawing him towards her both physically and emotionally this morning and now... here they were. It was still only six a.m. The foster family had arrived early to take baby Sahil away into their care, and he'd got the feeling that Ally didn't want to be alone.

Ally sat fiddling with the hem of her shirt

sleeve. 'So strange,' she agreed, her throat tight. 'I'm going to miss him so much. Silly, really.'

'Not silly,' he assured her, reaching for her hand, and letting them fall into a companionable silence, the kind that was probably only shared, he thought now, by those who had to do things like this for a living, on pretty much a daily basis. A lot had happened in the week since they'd rescued the jaundiced, abandoned newborn. Ally and he had visited him in the makeshift nursery every day, either together or separately, and he knew she'd grown attached. They both had. Not just to the baby, but to each other. And now, five weeks into her stint in Kerala it felt more as though she'd been away, and with Dev, for years. The air between them was charged and electric with the potential for something more than they'd ever discussed, because it was completely illogical to even think about it.

Dev cleared his throat, glancing at Ally. Her auburn hair was spilling over her shoulders like a cascade of leaves and he liked her with no makeup like this. He liked her…he just liked her. Too much.

'You know…' he began tentatively, his heart pounding against his ribcage as if trying to break free, 'you would make a fantastic mother some day.' His words floated into the space between them, landing softly yet resoundingly in the quiet of the tent. He'd been thinking it every time he'd seen her with Sahil, and even before that. 'It's what you want, right? Eventually, one day, if you meet the right person?'

She lowered her gaze. 'I doubt it will happen now, so it doesn't matter what I want.'

'You could meet someone,' he said.

Ally's gaze darted away, and Dev kicked himself. What was he doing? He could see the muscles in her jaw tighten. He recognised the evasion. It was clear she didn't want to unravel the threads of this conversation, not when their time together was a ticking clock. Valentine's Day, and Roisin's memorial, was just a week away. Why did he ask that anyway? It wasn't any of his business, they weren't in anything serious, and right now, each second was marching them closer to an inevitable goodbye. Everything he did was for Roisin. He owed it to Roisin's memory to keep moving, keep doing good in the world…to make up for what he inadvertently did to his family.

Ally met his eyes again and, for a moment, Dev saw a spark of her usual fire flicker back to life. Then her lips curved into a soft smile that did funny things to his insides. 'We're not here to think about stuff like that, are we?' she said, pressing a hand to his thigh and squeezing it suggestively. 'We promised we would make the most of now.'

'*Now*, now?' he asked, as his body reacted instantly.

Their gazes stayed locked tight. Dev could hear Ally's breath hitch ever so slightly, the pull between them was mutual. 'Ally,' he whispered, the name feeling like a caress even as it passed his lips. The rest of the world seemed to fall away as their hands found each other, fingers intertwining naturally. He brushed a strand of her hair away from her face. How could he lose this—her smile, the sound of her laughter that could somehow make a day's worth of exhaustion evaporate?

Ask her to stay, the voice in his head urged, suddenly. He should just ask her...but wouldn't that prove his selfishness? His life was a series of departures and destinations strung together, fleeting connections. How could he even try and tether Ally to such a transient existence when she seemed so content with this being a two-month thing?

'Dev, make love to me,' she murmured now, the syllables heavy with an emotion he couldn't even name. He was hardly going to refuse. He peeled off her shirt, and she unbuttoned his, aching to feel her skin against his, as much as possible. He tugged at her lip softly with his teeth, making her moan and arch into him.

How many times had they done this now? He was losing track. Every night, every morning, whenever they could sneak away. Ally's presence was a balm to the part of him that felt perennially adrift and he was starting to need her and crave her. But the thought of anchoring himself to her, only to inevitably sail away again left him stuck. She wouldn't want him, or this life, after a while, and he'd be the one to suffer. Dev's heart thudded against his ribcage as Ally arched into his touch. His hands knew her now, his fingers were expert navigators already when it came to her body.

'Is this OK?' Dev found himself asking, though every fibre of his being screamed for him to close the distance even further.

'More than OK,' Ally replied, her voice a whisper that somehow filled the tent. Their lips were dancing their regular dance now, even as he fought his mind to stop dragging up the past. The air between them crackled with anticipation, their breath mingling in the small canvas space, all longing and zero restraint. He could see the pulse quicken at the base of her throat as she ran her tongue over her lips. She was so beautiful.

'I think I'm—'

'Shh,' she said, placing a finger gently against his lips, her touch setting off a cascade of goosebumps across his skin. 'Don't,' she urged, but there were tears pooling in her eyes as he pressed into her and they moved as one. What was happening to him? This kind of thing just…did not happen to him. This was what he had feared, that he'd start falling in love with her, and want to change his entire lifestyle, when he'd sworn never to get this emotionally tangled again—no good could come of it. He had work to do, people all over the world to help, and how could he do that with integrity when his mind was wandering elsewhere?

But the longer they spent together the world around them—the canvas walls of the tent, the distant hum of the insects—all his self-imposed limitations receded into nothingness. There was only Ally: the curve of her waist under his hands, the silkiness of her hair as his fingers threaded through it, the press of her body against his, her fingers tracing the line of his jaw before tangling in his hair.

As they both reached the inevitable peak of pleasure, Ally muffled her cries into his shoulder and silenced his own with her hot mouth, and yet they still didn't stop. He lay inside her, wrapped around her, lost in her, and he was about to let out a laugh at the pure intensity, the crazy, unthinkable words that had actually been on the verge of tumbling out of his mouth, when suddenly, a huge jolt shook the entire tent.

Ally almost fell from the bed. Dev caught her, pulling her against him as the ground beneath

them started to shake violently, as though a giant
had reached from the sky, picked them up and
dropped them again. The tremor rippled through
the tent and outside, the sound of heavy objects
crashing and frightened screams sending a bolt
of panic through him. 'Earthquake!' Ally yelled
out in unison, her voice laced with panic. She
tried to jump off the bed of her own accord but
he stopped her.

'Wait, Ally, it might happen again.'

The chaos of the shaking world seemed to mirror the utter strangeness and unpredictability of
life he'd just been musing on, the fact that his
foundations were being truly shaken to the core
by this woman. Was this some kind of cosmic
joke?

'Are you all right?' he managed to ask over the
din of rattling medical supplies and the distant
cries of people in the vicinity who had just been
rocked awake by the quake.

'Yes, yes, I'm fine,' Ally breathed out, blinking
in shock. 'We have to make sure no one is hurt.'

They hurried to pull on their clothes and stumbled out of the tent as another aftershock from
the earthquake pulsed through the earth under
their feet. They had to get out, see who needed
help. What if someone was trapped? Ally's grip
on Dev's arm was vice-like, her knuckles white.
One minute they'd been making love and he'd

said…or almost said he loved her. Or had he? Nothing made sense right now.

She glanced around to see a member of the NHF team standing in the doorway of the next tent, looking shaken and sleepy, and now eyeing them with curiosity. The quake had subsided but now people, not just this guy, were seeing the two of them emerging from the same tent. But with the ground still threatening to split open at any moment, the potential for gossip was the least of Ally's concerns.

'Are you OK?' Dev called over, his voice steady despite the chaos erupting around them.

'I'm OK,' the guy said, swiping his brow. A quick ask-around confirmed no one was hurt. Ally could barely think straight.

'You OK?' Dev was looking at her again, concern written all over his face.

'Fine,' Ally managed to reply, though her voice trembled. She released his arm, suddenly conscious of how close they were standing together amidst the disarray.

As if on cue, the ground lurched beneath them again. 'Oh, God!' she squeaked, grabbing his arm again—who cared what anyone thought? A nearby table laden with medical supplies toppled over as the campsite descended into pandemonium. Glass vials shattered against the dirt, spilling their contents. A portable ultrasound machine crashed to the ground across the campsite, its screen flickering before going dark. Boxes of sterile gloves burst open, their contents scattering like bulky blue confetti. Ally's heart raced as she scanned the camp. A metal tray clanged loudly as it hit the floor, sending instruments skittering across the ground. The first-aid kits were upended, their bandages and antiseptics now covered in dust and debris. She heard something, coming from across the site. A person? Her heart lurched. Suddenly she was on her feet, heading for the noise.

'Watch out!' Dev called out sharply, yanking her back, just as the canvas roof of the nearby supply tent sagged dangerously, threatening to give way under the weight of a broken support beam.

'We need to see who's over there,' she cried, pointing to where she'd heard the noise. Her mind was spinning like a boat on the edge of a swirling vortex in the middle of the ocean, but she took several deep breaths, channelling calm. This was no time for hesitation or doubt. People could be injured and there could be more aftershocks coming.

'If you heard something, we'll go, but be careful, go slowly,' he implored, his own experience kicking in. She trusted him, she realised. Implic-

itly. But whether or not she trusted the ground
not to open up was a different story.

'We need to do another headcount,' Dev said,
his brown eyes scanning the area with a practised calm that totally belied the adrenaline that
must have been coursing through him as well.
The last headcount was already insignificant—
that last quake had been much more unsettling.

He gripped her hand as they made their way
towards the nursery, her heart thudding wildly.
Feeling his fingers curling into hers took her back
to just now...which already felt like months ago.
Had he really been about to confess something?
He was either about to climax or tell her he was
falling in love with her and the latter could hardly
be true, this drifter, this nomad who'd been vocally adamant that he'd never fall in love for any
reason. Why had she cut him off?

Another small sound pulled her focus back
to the present. They needed to act fast. Nothing
else mattered. Whatever almost-confessions had
been on the brink of being shared before all this
would have to wait. For now, there were lives at
stake, and she still couldn't see further than a
few feet in front of her without having to climb
over something.

Dev stayed one step ahead as they neared
the nursery. On the perimeter a few other people were trying to reach them, but he instructed

them all to stand back for now. Their ex-jaundiced baby, Sahil, was safe in the hands of his foster carers but there were others inside. Ally was wracking her brain, trying to recall who had stayed in there this morning. One young mother, and a newborn, she remembered now.

'Oh, Dev.' Ally's heart hammered in her chest as the high-pitched wails of infants cut through the clamour just ahead. Dev moved a heavy unit from her path and, without a second thought, she dashed the rest of the way to the nursery, her sneakers skidding on the dusty ground, strewn with baby bottles and formula. Somehow she navigated through the disarray, sidestepping a fallen examination lamp and shoving aside a toppled IV stand. Her mind briefly flashed to Dev's face just moments before the quake, his lips parting, eyes so intense she could barely stand it. It was so surreal, all of it.

A particularly loud cry snapped Ally back to reality. There she was. The young mother, her dishevelled hair clinging to her sweaty forehead, clutched her newborn close to her chest. Both of their bodies were covered in a thin layer of grey dust, making it difficult to tell where their clothing ended and the dust began. Without hesitation, Ally scooped up a first-aid kit that had miraculously fallen close by and approached them.

'Are you hurt?' she asked, and the woman

shook her head, holding out her baby now as if
she wasn't actually sure. Her baby, wrapped in
a dirty cloth, had a head full of wispy hair and
his eyes were wide, just as Oliver's had been,
when he'd been born. She had fallen in love with
her nephew on the spot. They didn't seem hurt,
thankfully, just scared.

'Come on, let's get you out of here,' she instructed, her voice firm but gentle. She turned
around, expecting Dev. But he wasn't there. A
knot formed in her stomach as she looked again,
hoping for a glimpse of his tall frame or the familiar sight of his dark hair. Where had he gone?
Another voice met her ears.

'Ally?' It was Raj, a volunteer. She instructed
him to help her guide the mother and child outside, checking for other people in the nursery on
the way. They'd been so lucky that more people
hadn't been in here! Outside, the knot in her belly
wound tighter and tighter as she searched the
campsite. People had straightened a lot of things
out already, but there was an air of tension and
mild shock amongst the locals, and she learned
that some of their kids were not yet accounted for.

'Pritya, have you seen Dev?' she asked a
nearby volunteer, who was busy securing a splint
on someone's leg.

'No, sorry,' she replied, not looking up from
her task.

'Has anyone seen Dev?' Ally called out, her voice barely cutting through the chaos. Each passing second without a sighting of him caused the knot to bind so tight she thought she might be ill and stop breathing altogether.

Forcing herself to focus, she saw to a minor cut on a young boy's leg, while she was informed that some people had gone to look for the missing children. He would have gone with them. She knew it. He had to be here somewhere. They needed all hands on deck, but more than that, she realised as she fought to keep the panic away, she needed him—his calmness, his expertise, his presence. She couldn't shake the fear that was latching onto her like a strangling device at the thought of him being hurt, or worse. *Not again, not again—please.*

'Ally!' A voice cut through the noise, strong and reassuring, instantly stilling her spiralling thoughts.

Oh, thank you, thank you.

It was Dev, emerging from around the tents that were still standing. A smear of dirt was streaked across his cheek but otherwise he seemed unharmed. Relief washed over Ally like a warm wave, and she almost laughed at the absurdity of feeling such profound gratitude, simply because he was OK. He wasn't Matt, he wasn't going to die on her…well, she hoped not anyway.

'Thank goodness you're OK.' She exhaled, not realising she'd been holding her breath.

'Of course I am,' he said, stepping closer. He almost wrapped his arms around her, she could see him itching to do it, just as she was, but she refrained. 'I see you got the mother and baby out... I was called off to help...'

'With the search, I know. Any luck?'

'Not yet. There are three of them. Rahul... Soman... Dinesh. They were last seen playing together right before the quake. They woke up early and said the dogs were acting weird, so they followed them outside. That's what their mothers told us.'

'Animals can sense these things coming,' she heard herself say, though her voice sounded as if it were coming from somewhere outside herself now. Those kids. What if they were hurt?

CHAPTER TWELVE

THE SEARCH WAS ON. The NHF workers and the locals split into groups. Ally and Dev took a road into the jungle, where they'd gone to see the elephants before. The kids often played around here and Ally could see the faint footprints of children and animals imprinted in the mud, leading in various directions. There was no sign of them though.

'It's so still. The birds have gone quiet,' she noted, and Dev nodded thoughtfully.

'So eerie.'

The road through the jungle was narrow and winding, surrounded by dense vegetation and towering trees. The leaves rustled in the wind, and rays of sunlight peeked through the canopy above them, now that it was after dawn. It would be hot again soon. The kids probably had no water, wherever they were. The occasional movement in the bushes made Ally's heart skip a beat, and another small tremor shook the ground beneath them, gently this time, though it still sent a ripple of panic through her belly, adding to the already tense atmosphere. Then…cries for help echoed out at them, sharp and desperate.

'Over there!' Dev was already on the move. She found herself praying as they raced towards the sound, the adrenaline fuelling their movements. Ally never prayed, but she could see the distress in Dev's eyes. Did he replay that night with his sister, in the car, every time there was an emergency situation like this? Every time there was a chance that he wouldn't be able to help?

He must carry every loss so deeply, as she did, as if it were his own. She might have gone some way to helping him see that he needed to let his family in, to stop inflicting more pain on them and himself by blocking them out of his life, but he still blamed himself for what had happened. It broke her heart that he did, but maybe it wasn't something you could just switch off after letting it rule your life for so long. It wasn't as if she could ever switch off her need to be near Nora and Oliver, not while they needed her.

An anguished scream suddenly pierced the air, halting them in their tracks. Dev spun around on the spot, holding a hand out in front of her to keep her quiet, and she strained her ears, listening for it again. 'Where are you?' he yelled out, and the seconds before they heard anything else seemed to last an eternity.

'Help!' It came again.

'I think I know where they are,' Ally said now, remembering the hunter's lodge from before. Dev seemed to read her mind, and she sprinted at his side through the dense brush, trying to force the thought of deadly creatures and big cat attacks from her mind.

The cabin was not the same place they'd been to before. At least it didn't look the same at all. Dev got on the radio to share the location while Ally got to her knees where the entrance used to be, near where Dev had found her that day when she'd been hiding from the kids. The metal structure had buckled and twisted under the force of the upheaval. Ragged sheets of corrugated iron had crumpled like tin foil and patches of rust were smudged with drifts of dirt and grit. The whole battered construct looked as if it had folded in on itself.

A sickening lump formed in her throat as she and Dev took in the wreckage. He crouched low, called the children's names, and they answered, giving whoops of joy that told her at least they weren't too hurt. But still, three young children were trapped inside this awful metallic carcass, their hopes pinned on her and Dev!

Just then, a small hand forced its way out from below the place the doorway used to be. Ally touched the boy's grubby fingers lightly. 'Hey, it's OK, we're here to help,' she said.

'Can you wiggle your fingers for me?' Dev asked. The children obeyed, and one by one they stuck their hands under, till a row of tiny digits wriggled in the dusty air. Relief washed over Ally. No crushed limbs—a very good sign.

'Can you tell me your names?' Dev added, looking to her. She knew he was trying to keep the children engaged while they worked out a plan. The narrow gap left after the collapse wasn't much more than a sliver but it was their only way in.

'It's Nurse Ally. I'm here with Dr Chandran,' she called into the dark recesses, keeping her voice steady despite the adrenaline coursing through her veins. 'We're going to get you out.'

She turned back to Dev, met his gaze a moment as her mind whirred. His brown eyes were hard with resolve. Without a word he started showing her what she should do to help, keeping his voice low or simply giving a nod here or there so as not to scare the kids inside. Together, they moved a lot of debris, communicating with silent movements that to anyone looking on, would make it pretty clear they'd been doing a lot more than just working professionally side by side recently.

They had become more than a team. As Dev lifted a plank, Ally supported it from the other end, the muscles in her arms protesting under the strain. Maybe it was the heat now forcing a trickle of sweat to slide down her back, maybe it was this unexpected disaster, but on top of knowing Dev was leaving her soon she couldn't help feeling far too emotional as they lifted, dug and extracted what they could from the scene.

'Ally, we need to move this section here—it's pinning down that corner,' Dev directed, indicating a twisted sheet of metal that had curled around a support beam like some kind of serpent.

'Push against my count,' he said, and she braced herself, thinking of the kids, ready to exert every ounce of strength she possessed. Dev's nose wrinkled up. 'One, two, three!' With a collective heave, they shifted the metal so there was just enough space to pull the children out. Only just as they moved it, another slab of metal crashed down, seemingly from nowhere. The kids all screeched, and it was all Ally could do not to scream herself.

'Are you hurt, Dev?'

'I'm OK.'

'Are you all OK in there?' she called out, resorting to prayers yet again inside her head. What was left of the roof sagged ominously, threatening to collapse further at any moment.

'We're good,' came the reply.

'I can't move this piece…can you work around me?' Dev said now.

'I'll try!'

In a feat that surely should have seen him donning some kind of superhero's cape first, Dev supported the heavy shard of metal on his back, his face taut with the weight of it, while Ally gently lifted one of the frightened children from beneath it. This was the eldest boy, Rahul. She recognised him.

'Can you hold it?' she asked Dev, frightened he would drop it at any moment. 'Careful with that—it looks jagged,' Ally warned, as she and Rahul both tried to help move it aside. It was no good, the thing was locked between Dev, more trees and obstinate branches.

'It's fine, keep them coming,' he urged them.

'Please, help my brother and my friend,' Rahul pleaded, but Ally was already reaching in carefully to try and get the next child out—a boy no older than seven. This was Soman.

'Come to me, sweetheart,' Ally coaxed, extending her arms. Soman hesitated before allowing himself to be guided into the tiny space. He was heavy despite his small size, and clearly couldn't hoist himself out as well as Rahul had, but together they managed to get him far enough through the new gap, as Dev grunted close by. 'You OK?' she checked in.

'Mmmph,' came his reply.

Oh, gosh, she had to move faster. Poor Dev.

The third child, a little younger but trying hard to be brave, clung to a tattered stuffed elephant. Ally reached for him with open arms. 'I'll take care of Mr Trunk too, Dinesh,' she promised, and the scared child let out a quivering breath that was almost but not quite a cry as he bravely let go, surrendering the toy to her care. As quickly as she could, Ally managed to extricate him. His small body was trembling all over, but thankfully he wasn't injured. It was a miracle these kids had only minor scratches, considering the state of the structure that had collapsed on them.

Just as Dev finally allowed what was left of the corrugated wall to drop to the ground, the crunch of leaves and debris behind them made them turn. Raj was here again, waving the radio. In the distance, the whine of a rescue truck told them more help was finally here. At last, they'd been able to get a vehicle around the debris.

'Everything's going to be fine. You were so brave,' she whispered, more to herself than to the children. The dust had caked onto all of their bodies, turning their torn clothes a ghostly grey. Scratches criss-crossed their skin, and now she realised that Rahul had a deep gash on his arm that he'd failed to mention before helping them rescue the others. Dev spotted it just as she did.

'Careful with that arm,' Dev warned in a hushed tone, and he got to his knees, checking for signs of fracture.

'I'm OK, Doctor,' the boy insisted, and Ally nodded, quickly disinfecting it with the kit she had thankfully brought from the nursery.

'You're a real hero, you know that,' she told him, casting her eyes to Dev right after. He could have been crushed just now, but he'd taken on the challenge willingly, put himself second.

'We heard there's a missing dog, still,' Raj said now.

'Boop ran away. He was scared.' The kid with the elephant sniffled, and Ally crossed to him again, brushed his dirty cheeks kindly with her equally dirty fingers. She felt a hot pang of missing Oliver. She would lose her mind, knowing something like this had happened to him and his friends.

'We'll keep looking for your dog,' she said, turning to Raj. 'Please inform their mothers they're safe.'

'He will,' Dev replied on his behalf. He was at her side now, and he took her hand, not caring, apparently, if Raj was literally standing in front of them. A small smirk of knowing crossed Raj's face, and, without a word, he led the kids away back towards the campsite.

'OK, let's think this through,' Dev said when

the crunch of their shoes was out of ear shot. He looked terrible now, and so did she, probably. Hot, dirty, exhausted. 'If you were a dog, where would you go?'

'I'd go towards the camp,' she said, after a moment. 'Or to the village, where there's food and water.'

'He wasn't at the camp, we would have heard,' he said, leading her in the other direction.

Together they made their way in the hot sun towards the local village. It was about a mile from the campsite, but there were paths and trails a dog might have taken along the way if it was seeking shelter. Dev was exhausted and he knew his back must be black and blue under his shirt from holding that sheet up. He handed Ally a bottle of water he'd got from Raj and she drank from it thirstily, as if she'd never had water in her entire life. Dev called out for the missing dog, knowing full well there might be more people who needed help too. Who knew the extent of things in the village?

Today was crazy. This morning felt like a thousand years ago already. Did he really stop himself from saying he loved Ally, right as they'd been…well, making love? He'd been unpacking this ever since. The way his mouth had tripped up, followed by the pounding of knowing in his chest, and his swollen heart. Maybe she thought he'd been about to say something entirely different, he thought, realising what an idiot he would have been to tell her something like that in the heat of the moment. Even though he meant it. He had somehow fallen for this woman, one hundred per cent completely. But how could they have anything lasting? Was he even capable of it, even if she was? Life was different already with her in it, and it wasn't going to be easy to give up, but this was all unprecedented, and he still wasn't sure what to do.

Ally's hand gripped his as they took the path into the village and a pained cry hit their ears. It was coming from one of the small shacks that passed for houses. A woman.

'Over there!' Ally cried out, her legs already propelling her forward. Dev was at her side in an instant.

The air was thick with dust and panic as the harrowed cries led them to the tiny building. It was barely clinging to its definition of a home; the ceiling drooped threateningly like the shack they'd just pulled the kids from, and the surrounding walls were fractured mosaics of plaster and children's drawings.

'We're here,' Ally announced as she hurried ahead of him, sweeping aside a fallen chair to reveal the woman, cowering under a chipped wooden table. Her face was slick with sweat and contorted in pain. She couldn't have been more than sixteen, with a tumble of raven hair spread around her like a fan. Her dark eyes were wide with fear and they latched onto Dev's as they approached. The girl's body heaved with contractions, her hands clutching the tattered remnants of what must have been a colourful sari just an hour or so ago, but it was so dusty he could hardly make out any colours now.

Dev's heart jumped like a giant grasshopper in his throat as he navigated the fallen debris in the direction of the tap, his unsteady steps echoing out on the hard concrete floor. Quickly he refilled his water bottle and took it to the lady, instructing her to drink.

'We need to keep calm,' Ally was saying as he knelt beside the expectant mother who was grimacing in pain, sucking in huge breaths one after the other. 'Find whatever blankets and towels you can. Let's make her comfortable and prepare for delivery,' Ally said. 'The trucks won't be able to get here for a while. It took us long enough on foot.'

He followed her instructions, moving swiftly to a rickety wooden cabinet standing crooked in a corner and pulling open the drawers. His fingers wrapped around several fluffy towels folded neatly together. Some were small hand towels while others were larger bath sheets.

'Dev?' Ally was holding out her arms and he walked to her.

'Focus,' he murmured to himself, shaking off the memories and self-doubt. He realised his mind had flipped to a time at his grandma's house when he and Roisin had played hide and seek in the linen closet. He could picture her now with him; he and Roisin had been so close. If the dead really did watch over you, was she here now, cheering him on as he and Ally did everything in their power to ensure this baby's safe arrival into the world? What did she think of Ally? he wondered. Did she love her as much as he did?

He caught himself again, helping Ally disperse the sheets and blankets, creating a sort of bed to ease the woman's discomfort. This woman was throwing him into chaos, earthquake or not, and he'd almost told her he loved her this morning! Crazy. *But you have started to fall in love with her,* he thought, watching her holding the young woman's hand, encouraging deep, long breaths through another contraction. This kind of blossoming love had crept up slowly, born from respect and mutual understanding and, yes, the pain they had both had to endure before being thrown together like this. He would spend the rest of his life wondering what Ally was doing, and who with, if it wasn't him.

He saw the unwavering strength in her now, the same resilience that made her an anchor for her family back home. Ally was too rooted in her world to ever be swept up by his nomadic life. While his existence was a series of temporary stops in far-flung corners of the globe, Ally's soul was tethered to her loved ones, to Oliver, who adored her, to Nora, her sister, who relied on her. And he couldn't risk his life's work on a romance. It was too important; this was his legacy, in honour of Roisin. After he'd failed her and his family like that, he barely even deserved a great love anyway.

'Dev, it's going to happen, soon,' she said, barely flinching as the girl squeezed her hand till the colour drained right out. They had no oxygen for her, nothing.

The young mother whimpered, her face ashen with fear and exhaustion already. She looked impossibly young beneath the grime and sweat. Dust motes danced in the slanted light that was piercing through a crack in the wall. This would surely be all over the international news by now. Was his family worried about him? Did they ever worry they might lose him too, as they'd lost Roisin? Dev steadied himself as the young woman let out a wail that by all rights should have created another shockwave through the village. Somewhere in the distance a dog barked. Ally's eyes met his and he knew she was thinking the same thing. Was it the dog they'd come looking for? No time to look now.

'Can you imagine what Nora's thinking right now? Hearing about the earthquake on the news?' Ally's voice trembled slightly as the woman stilled between contractions. He frowned. Of course she had been thinking it too. 'She must be out of her mind with worry.'

'Let's give her some good news to hear about once we're out of here,' he replied, throwing a reassuring smile her way that he was sure didn't quite reach his eyes. Of course she was thinking about her sister—she was always thinking about her family. He was just selfish, he realised. That fact was undeniable. It hit him as if the roof had come down on him, and this time, he let himself be burdened with it, feeling it crush him slowly.

'You're doing great. Just focus on your breathing, all right?' he encouraged. Ally positioned herself behind the woman now, letting her lean back against her chest. She brushed damp strands of hair from her forehead, murmuring words of comfort as her breaths grew more ragged with exertion. He did not deserve this woman, for so many reasons, but their teamwork was seamless by now, a fluid exchange. What was he going to do, once she was back in the UK and he was... who knew?

'Dev, I need you to support her legs,' Ally instructed now. It was hot, getting hotter by the moment in this enclosed space, and in moments the baby was crowning. 'All right,' Ally continued, her blue eyes fixed on the emerging head of the baby. 'When I say push, you help her lift slightly, OK? On my count... One, two, three—push!'

Dev was as prepared as he could be as the woman, this terrified mother-to-be-any-moment-now, caught in the throes of labour, bore down with all her might, pushing her weight so far back into Ally she almost toppled over backwards. 'Good, good,' Ally encouraged anyway. 'Just a bit more.'

The supplies they had were meagre—a few clean cloths, a small bowl of water he'd brought from the tap in the corner, and the same basic first-aid kit they'd brought from camp, which seemed laughably inadequate for the task at hand, but if Ally was daunted by it all being so drastically different from what the midwives dealt with in Somerset she wasn't conveying that to this woman at all.

'Another push,' she instructed, signalling for him to switch places with her. After one more agonised cry from the woman, Ally gently cradled the newborn's head and shoulders, easing the tiny being into the world, slick and wailing right away, as if it…he, or she…was protesting already.

'You have a healthy baby girl.' Ally breathed out, a smile spreading across her face as she wrapped the baby carefully in a clean sheet. Pure adrenaline surged like lightning through his veins as he took the newborn from Ally's careful grip, feeling for the pulse at the tiny wrist, counting under his breath, relieved at the strong, regular rhythm. They would have to make do with palpation and observation in lieu of stethoscopes and monitors until they could get them to the hospital but so far, miraculously, everything seemed well.

'Good heart rate,' he murmured, more to himself than to Ally, who was sponging the woman's brow with cool water. Dev wrapped the baby again in another brightly coloured sari he'd found in the drawer, quickly repurposing it into a swaddling blanket.

He felt Ally's eyes on him as he did it, and when he looked up, she was still watching. Her eyes held a different kind of light as she observed him with the baby, and for a second he wondered what she was thinking. Picturing him as a dad, as Cassinda had? The thought had all but turned his stomach back then. But now, for some reason, the thought didn't feel quite so alien. He'd done more difficult things in his time. Spending all that time with the abandoned baby, Sahil, had changed something, made him think that, with the right woman, maybe he could do this too one day. Of course, then the demons raced back in, reminding him otherwise.

Gently he handed the infant to her mother. His eyes met Ally's again over the tiny bundle, and something passed between them before she quickly looked away with a small harried sigh. In that moment, the pull towards Ally was almost impossible to ignore and suddenly he thought he might ask her to come to Canada with him. But then what? She hadn't specifically said she wanted marriage, kids, a man to settle down with, but she'd been planning all that with her ex who died, so it was written in her stars. Not for him though…not for him, never. He didn't deserve those things, at the end of the day, and his missions with the NHF were more important.

He leaned against the cool, cracked wall, radioed in what they'd done. Ally gently cleaned the mother's forehead again with a damp cloth while she cradled her baby, suddenly lost in wonder and joy. What a start in life, he thought. What a way to come into the world!

The air was still thick with the metallic scent of blood and he could hear the distant wail of sirens growing louder now. Help was coming. Just as he was about to help them both up to head outside, a noise from the doorway pulled his attention back.

'Oh, hi,' Ally said from behind him. 'Heard all the noise, did you?'

The dog was standing there, a scruffy caramel-coloured mutt with a patch of white fur over one eye. Dev was sure he recognised it—it was the dog they'd been looking for, the one belonging to the boys.

'So you found us before we could find you, huh, buddy?' he said with a sigh. Its tail wagged tentatively as it padded over the threshold and into the dishevelled room, nose twitching, dark eyes wide with curiosity. It paused for a moment, head cocked to one side as it assessed the situation. Dev watched as Ally stretched out a hand, inviting the dog to come closer for a sniff, and with her encouragement the dog finally took the last few steps and pressed its cold nose into Ally's open palm, right before nudging softly at the baby's foot, making the young mother laugh. They all laughed as its tail started wagging faster in excitement. Finally, a moment of normality in a morning that so far had been so surreal.

Things were going to be OK, he thought with relief. Thanks to Ally. Well, thanks to both of them, another kid had been given a fighting chance amidst a tragedy. It was just a shame that all this had cemented his own place in the world, a selfish man hiding out in the guise of a hero.

An escape artist, playing the role of a stable lover and partner.

Ally deserved more. She might not realise it now, but when she came down from this high, she'd see that this agreement they'd made had some dangerous hidden clauses. Falling in love with Ally was ruining him already but he would only make things worse for both of them if they carried this on. From now on, he decided, he had to be less selfish in general, starting with letting her go.

CHAPTER THIRTEEN

THE STERILE WHITE cotton kept blurring in her vision as Ally folded the bandages. Of course, she was still thinking about the quake and everything they'd endured, but Dev had retreated emotionally. It was as if he'd already boarded that plane, in his head, and flown back to Canada. The base camp was like a buzzing beehive with the NHF volunteers all rushing about, but the echo of that young mother's relieved sobs and the baby's first cry after they'd helped it enter the world three whole days ago kept springing back to her mind, too, drowning out the commotion. She should have felt elated for having saved them, for finding those children and the dog, but a hollow unease had settled in her chest since. Nothing could get rid of it. And it was all because of Dev's sudden distance.

Ever since the team had been relocated back to base camp following the quake, he'd been someone else completely, as if he were pulling back the parts of himself he had given her piece by tiny piece, until she was left wondering if he'd ever given her anything at all. If she'd imagined it.

Grabbing her water bottle, she perched on the edge of the bench by the door, her eyes tracing the patterns of dust kicked up by all the passing feet. Zoning out. Since the earthquake, Dev had been like a ghost around her, his usual warm brown eyes somewhere far, far away. Someone had hung paper hearts around the place ahead of the party, or 'Celebration of Love', that was happening later tonight. Valentine's Day wasn't so much of a thing around here as it was back home, but the volunteers from their respective places around the world were throwing a little party early, anyway, before being assigned to the next mission. Everyone needed a break after the panic of the quake, and the clean-up. Would Dev even attend the party? she wondered. Or would he stay in his hotel room as he had the past few nights?

Ally couldn't help but wonder if his withdrawal was because of what had almost slipped out of his mouth that morning. The almost-confession still lingered between them. He probably hadn't meant it at all, he'd just been caught up in the moment…unless he *had* meant it, and he was just as freaked out by the implications as she was. A future was impossible, they both knew it. They wanted different things. Still, the knot tightened in her stomach as she considered the possibility of leaving Kerala without understanding where they stood.

'Ally?' Dev's voice sliced through the drone of conversation around them.

She glanced up to find him standing in front of her suddenly, his dark eyes brewing with an intensity that made her pulse quicken. His shirt was buttoned all the way to the top again, as it had been that first day. For some reason it irked her now, made him seem even more closed off to her, buttoning himself back up so she couldn't reach him.

'Are you going to this party later?' he asked her simply.

'I suppose so,' she replied. Her heart was stuttering, even as she attempted to sound nonchalant. He nodded, but before he could say anything else, Dr Anjali Kapur diverted their attention. Her trademark flowing sari was a rainbow as usual and her smile was as enchanting as ever as she floated over to them.

'Spencer,' Anjali said, extending a piece of paper towards her. 'Your new assignment.'

Ally took the sheet, scanning the typed text. She was being sent to a small village in Rajasthan, where a waterborne disease outbreak needed urgent attention. Her role would be critical, leading health education efforts and supporting local nurses. Exciting. Challenging, probably. The perfect end to her mission in India…but what about Dev? Would he be assigned anything or was he still going to leave and fly back to Canada ahead of the real Valentine's Day, also Roisin's birthday, and the day of her memorial? The plans had all been thrown out of whack after the quake.

'Sounds interesting, thank you. I'm excited for this one,' she managed to say with a tight smile.

'Your expertise is needed there, Spencer. You leave first thing tomorrow.' She looked between them. 'I hope that won't be a problem?'

Oh, gosh. Anjali knew about them. Word had got back that something had been going on anyway. It was hardly a secret, not since everyone had seen them leaving the same tent that morning.

'Thank you, I won't let you down,' Ally said, but hadn't she let her down already, breaking focus all those moments to lose herself in Dev? She'd let herself down anyway. Excitement was the furthest thing from what she felt now. But she plastered a smile onto her face as Anjali turned to Dev next. There was no piece of paper for him.

'Chandran? I understand you won't be continuing this assignment, that you're heading back to Canada for a while?' she said.

Ally's stomach dropped into a sloshy puddle despite her smile as Dev nodded his head subtly.

'I leave tomorrow, yes. I'm not sure how long for. Not for long, hopefully.'

'Spending time with your family is important. Take as long as you need,' Anjali followed, and Ally didn't miss the quick glance in her direction, from both of them this time. Ugh. Dev was still bowing out early. He wasn't taking another position. Not here, not anywhere else in India. So with her also shipping out in the morning, she might never see him again after this.

'Excuse me,' Ally uttered, her voice barely above a whisper. She needed air, space, something to anchor the swirling thoughts threatening to capsize her composure in front of all these people. She stood to walk away and head for the door, but Dev called out.

'See you tonight, Ally?'

'I'll see you there,' she told him, without turning back. It would be their last goodbye.

Her hotel room felt smaller than usual as she sat on the faded bedspread, the phone pressed to her ear. Larissa's voice was a beam of sunlight that pulled her from the storm in her head, as it always had, even though she seemed to be having issues of her own with Thor. Ally could tell her friend was developing real feelings too, and denying them. All she could do, when pressed for details on Dev, was bite her tongue, as if she could bite back her own crazy thoughts, now forming a knot in her stomach. She couldn't say it, for some reason. She couldn't say she had fallen in love with Dev. Because then it would be real. He was leaving anyway, ironically before Valentine's Day—a date that up till now had held absolutely zero significance aside from a few bunches of supermarket flowers from Matt when he'd remembered, and maybe a card.

Ally couldn't believe how complicated things were getting for Larissa either, over there in the polar winds with her Viking. To think, they'd both come on this adventure looking for a simple no-strings fling, and now...well, who knew? They ended the call with a promise to keep each other updated and Ally's gaze drifted to the window. A hummingbird hovered near a cluster of bright flowers outside, and she watched its wings beat with a rapid, frantic energy that looked a lot like how she felt every time she thought about Dev. Restless. As if she were hovering on the edge of something that was just out of reach.

There was no denying the connection they had, fragile as it might be. Even when he was being distant, she could feel him still inside her, seeping into her blood like sugar into water. The thought of facing him tonight sent a ripple of anticipation through her. But it also struck her dizzy with a fear she couldn't shake off. She thought of Matt, the way they used to crack themselves up over

stupid stuff, stuff that hadn't been funny to anyone else. Well, sometimes she'd been the only
one laughing, but still…

OK, so maybe he hadn't been perfect, and
maybe, now she really was being honest, she and
Dev were a better match physically, and mentally
too…but he'd loved her, and she'd loved him, so
much so that she hadn't made room for so much
as the thought of ever being with anyone else.
This thing with Dev was stirring up some element of guilt too, the more she thought about
it. Was she betraying Matt's memory? She definitely hadn't fallen for him as fast as she had
apparently fallen for Dev.

Whatever it was that seemed to be simmering
between them wasn't all stemming from the past.
Not her past, and not his either, she was sure of it.
It was its own entity—alive, unpredictable, and
demanding to be acknowledged. Larry had tried
to convince her that Nora and Oliver would be
fine without her there. But Larry was wrong, they
were not fine—how could they be fine? They did
need her. They would always need her.

'Maybe he can visit me,' she whispered to the
hummingbird, allowing the words to hang in the
air like the creature. 'Visit me in Frome.' The idea
sparked a flicker of hope, but she squeezed her
eyes shut, laughing at herself. As if Dev would
want to go to Frome!

But Larissa wouldn't forgive her if she didn't at least float the thought.

Ally felt his eyes on her the second she stepped from the palace terrace into the garden. How on earth they'd managed to secure such a venue was beyond her. It was literally fit for a king. The NHF had impressed some people over the last months, but right now, the only person she wanted to impress was Dev. He was talking to some other people and stayed in the conversation, but she felt his eyes trailing her as she clutched a single red rose and made her away around the garden towards her seat. The tables were illuminated by strings of fairy lights that cast a glow on the blooming flowers around the perimeter. The dark green foliage bent in the warm night breeze as if it were bowing to them and her heart drummed against her ribs as she stopped to talk to another volunteer.

'You look amazing, Ally, great dress. Red is your colour. Who's your rose for?'

'I don't know yet,' she replied. Ally cast her eyes sideways to Dev again. They had all been given a rose on the way in, and told to hand it to someone special. It didn't have to be anything romantic. Some people were laughing, handing them out to one another as friendly gestures, but Dev was still holding his to his side, just as she was.

'I think you do,' came the knowing reply, before the woman floated away, leaving Ally standing alone, rubbing her arms. Was it too late to back out? To head to her room and hide away? *No, chicken. Talk to him!*

Maybe she'd have one small glass of wine first, she thought, hoping it would calm her nerves. He was at the bar now anyway, talking to someone else. A woman. Jealousy flared in her chest for a moment before she reminded herself she was here with a mission. She had to be brave and talk to him. She was the one he'd been sleeping with, not this woman. There was no one else. It was just…everything else, getting in their way.

Ally's heart fluttered like one of the strung-up paper hearts as she approached the bar, trying to keep her cool. It was a beautiful set-up, trestle tables adorned with more flowers under the tree. But she barely noticed the decorations as she took a deep breath and walked over to them.

'Hey,' she greeted them both with a smile. Dev turned to her, his brown eyes widening in surprise. 'Ally! You look amazing.'

As if you didn't notice me before, she felt like saying. She felt herself blush at his compliment and smiled anyway. 'Thank you.'

The other woman excused herself, giving Ally

and Dev some privacy. She couldn't help wonder if everyone here knew that something had been going on, following their exit from that tent together. With time running out though, she couldn't exactly afford to address the issue of her depleting professionalism right now.

'So, who's your rose for?' Dev asked, gesturing towards the red flower in her hand.

She hesitated for a moment before finally admitting, 'For you.'

He nodded slowly, a slight smirk on one side of his handsome face. He looked so good tonight in yet another shirt buttoned up to the top and navy-blue dress trousers that matched his tie. 'Who's yours for?' she dared.

He lowered his eyes, then looked up at her through ink-black eyelashes. 'Who do you think?' he said, offering it in one palm. She couldn't help smiling as they swapped roses, both ending up with an almost identical flower, just like everyone else in the vicinity. 'Happy almost Valentine's Day,' he said.

Her dress suddenly felt too tight. It wasn't quite Valentine's Day yet. Not quite his sister's birthday. Just thinking about him leaving tomorrow for Canada made her heart shrink inside her till she was left reaching for the jug on the bar, suddenly dying of thirst.

'I just wanted to talk to you,' she said, touching a finger to her wet lips.

He frowned and loosened his tie a little, looking everywhere but her. 'I know, me too.'

Ally swallowed a golf ball from her throat. She lowered her voice, stepped a little closer. 'What's going on, Dev? I've missed you.'

Her heart was pounding. She'd never felt so vulnerable in her life, but as his eyes landed on hers again, she felt the most powerful surge of emotions that she could hardly keep from showing on her face. This was bravery though, this was facing it, she told herself, when everything inside had been warning her to run, to keep the barriers up, just as he was doing. He wasn't Matt. Matt had had no choice but to leave her. Dev was choosing to leave without making any plans to ever see her again. And this time she needed proper closure, one way or the other.

Before she knew it, he was taking her arm gently, and leading her away from the bar. They passed the crowds, back into the palace, where Dev tried several doors only to find them locked. They soon found themselves in the cloakroom, complete with a golden chandelier that was wasted on the tiny room of hooks and lockers. Dev pulled the lock across the door behind them.

'Ally,' he said, turning to her. He opened his

mouth to continue speaking but she interrupted him quickly.

'Can I ask you something?' Her voice was steady now, even if her heart was doing acrobatics inside her chest.

'Of course,' Dev replied, his hand tightening around the rose as he looked at her. All around them, scarves and shawls created an ocean of colour, but the room felt as if it were closing in.

'I know you have to go. I know that's probably why you've been distancing yourself, and I don't blame you, but would you consider…would you think about visiting me in the UK?' The words tumbled out of her, not as graceful as she had rehearsed in her head, but at least they were out.

Dev leaned back against the door, the surprise etched plainly across his features. It was as if she'd presented him with a puzzle, the pieces all scattered and uneven around them, and he'd been tasked with putting them together under the scrutiny of her hopeful gaze.

'Visit you?' he echoed, obviously buying himself time as he processed her request. Ally cringed. This was silly.

'Yes,' she said anyway, squeezing her rose so tight a thorn jabbed into her palm, making her drop it. She felt her fingers intertwining in a knot of anxious energy. 'I mean, no pressure. Just a visit. When I'm home, and you've spent some time with your family.'

She watched the play of emotions on his face—the furrow of his brow, the slight parting of his lips—as he weighed her words against whatever was going on in his head. She knew all too well the demons that danced in his mind, the fear of commitment that shadowed his every step since that thing with his colleague, Cassinda. His desire to remain untethered clashed with this undeniable connection that had grown between them, but he had to face it too, didn't he? Discuss it?

'Ally, that's…' Dev began, then paused, searching for the right words. 'It's a big step.'

Her heart sank. 'It's whatever it has to be, Dev.'

'I'll be taking the next assignment, wherever they send me,' he reminded her. She nodded, trying to steady her breathing and calm the storm of emotions that still threatened to spill over. It was as if every beat of her heart were tethered to his words now. He stepped forwards. 'And what will you do, Ally? Do you really still want to go back to England? It's not like you have to, you know. No one is forcing you. There's plenty of work with the NHF.'

His gaze pierced her, poking a hole in her armour. For a second she stared at him, floored. 'That's not part of the plan, Dev. My sister needs me. Oliver needs me. You know I have to go back. I don't have a choice.'

He shook his head slowly. 'I don't know if that's true.'

'It *is* true. Why wouldn't it be true?' she challenged. What was with everyone insinuating her place was not with Nora, who still needed her? 'But there's a lot of work in England. We could find you something, we could both find...'

'That's not part of the plan,' he repeated. He shook his head resolutely. 'And anyway, I thought we *both* agreed that this was a bit of fun.'

Ouch.

Embarrassment threatened to short-circuit her entire system as she stood there in front of him, wishing she could disappear. For a second it looked as if he was about to reach for her, but he pulled back at the last second, swiped his hands into his hair.

'I just don't want to make the same mistakes again,' he admitted, his gaze not wavering from hers, even as she looked away, swiping at her wet eyes.

'I get it. I'm just another Cassinda.' She couldn't exactly help the snarky tone, but it didn't mirror her hurt either—how could it?

The moment lingered as Dev chewed on his lower lip, his forehead set in a deep frown. Voices chattered in the distance, a man laughed nearby, and somewhere, a bell tinkled. But for Ally, the whole world narrowed down to the man standing across from her. Right now, this one guy held her hopes and her heart in his hands.

'I get it, Dev. You want to be free and single for ever, floating around the world!'

'Ally, we had an agreement.'

Oh, gosh, this was humiliating. She had sworn she would never be in this position, yet here she was, and he was letting her down gently.

'I thought you were going to say you loved me, the other morning, before the earthquake,' she managed, doing her best to stand tall. 'You were, weren't you…? And then you just went all ice man on me, like nothing ever happened.'

'I'm sorry,' he said, his voice steadier than she felt.

'You're sorry,' she muttered, almost kicking the rose across the floor, then reining in her sudden fury. This was not how she'd expected this to go. 'I'm sorry, Dev. I am so very sorry. I clearly misread the situation.'

'Ally…we want different things.'

'I know, but I don't know. I've never done this before, but we could work something out. We've both lost people in our lives, Dev. I'm not ready to lose you. There, I said it.'

A pained look crossed his face for just a second. Enough time to see the guarded expression in his eyes, and the weight he still carried on his shoulders—the weight of a guilt that wasn't his to bear. She reached out finally, her hands finding his. She could already feel him slipping away.

'You don't have to keep running from what happened with your sister, you know, and you don't have to deny yourself happiness because you feel guilty. The accident wasn't your fault. Is that what this is about, really? You're just going to keep moving around, throwing yourself into danger zones, wherever they send you?'

'It's what I enjoy, Ally.'

'It's not going to bring her back!'

His jaw clenched, the muscle twitching with the effort of holding back. He looked away over her shoulder and she bit down hard on her cheeks. She had to tell him, even if he still rejected her. If she didn't, she would always wonder what if. 'Dev, after Matt died, I never thought I could feel anything like this again, for anyone. But then I met you and everything changed. Everything! You reminded me of what it felt like to be happy and carefree…and I don't want to lose that. I don't want to lose someone else I love.'

Silence.

Still, nothing. She watched his face, the way his jaw tightened and his throat pulsed, as if he was swallowing something back that he didn't know how to say. Panic coiled in her belly. He wasn't saying anything. Gosh, she was being a total idiot. She was still waiting for him to say he loved her, that this fling had developed into something he couldn't lose, that he didn't want to lose her either.

'I don't feel the same,' he confessed instead.

Ally felt as if he'd slapped her. 'What?' she mumbled in shock, realising she was trembling, and cold. Goosebumps flared up her arms. 'But you almost said you lo—'

'No, I didn't,' he said, setting his mouth into a straight line, so unlike the way she'd had him memorised till now. Now, this was all she would remember. 'If I did, I was lost in the moment. Ally, we both got carried away. We agreed it would stop if it stopped being fun. So this is me, stopping it.'

With that, he turned around and fumbled with the door handle. In another second flat, he was gone, and Ally reached for her phone. She wouldn't break down, she would not. But she needed to call Larry immediately.

CHAPTER FOURTEEN

DEV'S NEPHEW, NIKKI, squealed in delight from his place on the couch next to him, his avatar leaping and ducking as the boy clutched the controller of the games console. On any other day, the playful shouts and laughter of his favourite kid in the whole world would have been contagious, but today, the joy seemed to ricochet off him. Not only was it Valentine's Day for real. A reminder of everything this family and this house had lost. He had ruined things with Ally and he just couldn't get her out of his head.

The delicious aroma of simmering spices wafted from the kitchen. His parents were preparing food for the memorial dinner and they were talking with each other, punctuating the air with the clatter of pots and pans ahead of the so-called celebration. All their friends were invited. Everyone who had ever known Roisin was invited to laugh and remember and cry, and the guests would arrive soon—friends, relatives, echoes of the past. He'd be forced to talk about her, and remember…everything.

'Uncle Dev, you just died again. Pay attention!' Nikki called out, pretending to bash him with his controller.

'Sorry, buddy,' he said.

'Your uncle's just jet-lagged, that's all,' his brother Romesh said, dropping a bunch of knives and forks on the table. 'Hey, Dev, beer run?'

'Definitely,' Dev replied, ruffling his nephew's hair and jumping up from the couch. Despite his outward focus on his brother as they drove into town, his mind was miles away in Kerala, with Ally. The thought of her watery blue eyes on that last day, brimming with tears over his cruelty, broke his heart. The loss of her sent an ache through him. He could almost hear her cracking a joke, trying to mask the pain that had always lingered just beneath the surface. How was she feeling now that he'd stolen his affections away… forced her to think she'd lost him that he'd never loved her in the first place? He had taken his selfishness to new levels by lying but he'd been trying to set her free of him.

His brother cast a sidelong glance at him from behind the wheel. 'Spill it. You've been more ghost than man today.'

Dev chuckled, but it sounded hollow. 'Sorry.

Just thinking about something. Someone,' he admitted.

'I knew it. Ally, huh?' Dev had mentioned her briefly on the drive back from the airport when Romesh had picked him up, but he'd found he couldn't quite talk about it all then. 'Come on, give me the dirt. What's got you so twisted up?'

Dev found himself clenching his fists, voicing thoughts he'd barely admitted to himself since storming out of that cloakroom and making his way back to the hotel. He'd left early the next morning, and spent the whole time in the departure lounge fighting the urge to turn back. 'I ended things. I didn't want to hold her back.'

'From what? Being happy with you?' His brother's teasing tone had shifted, edged with sincerity now.

'From her life in the UK. Her family needs her.' As he said it, he knew she would never change her mind about that. But he hadn't exactly done much to convince her that she had every right to stop holding herself back for the sake of everyone else. Just like him, perhaps?

Romesh's mouth formed a thin, hard line. 'Settling down hasn't really ever been your thing. We all know that.'

'Maybe not…but maybe she got me thinking about a few things,' Dev conceded, the words tasting bitter on his tongue. Fear had taken root deep inside his bones—a fear of falling for someone he could hurt or lose, a fear of failing someone else on the cusp of a life-or-death situation. But ever since he'd been home, his whole family had taken him in with open arms, his mother especially. He'd found her upstairs that first afternoon, looking through clothes in her wardrobe, and he'd walked up behind her, told her he was sorry. Sorry for hiding away, for being an emotionless black hole, for being so afraid of hearing her blame him that he'd stayed away longer than he should have. Slowly, she had turned to face him.

'Dev, I never wanted to hear you say that you thought I blamed you for the accident.' The words had tumbled out in a rush, and the dam had broken. His mother's composure had crumbled, and she'd sobbed, reaching for him. Dev had enveloped her in his arms, her tears dampening his shirt as he'd held her, and forced himself to let the guilt and shame wash over him until it was out of his system completely.

'Oh, my son,' she'd wept, 'I've never once blamed you. Not for a single moment.'

She'd talked about Roisin after that, brought up a hundred memories, and every time he'd felt only love. And in turn, his love for Ally had grown and grown till it felt as if it were strangling him from the inside. Why had it taken so long for him to process this…all of it?

'Look, Dev,' his brother said now as they pulled into the car park, 'no one's saying it's going to be easy. But I haven't seen you this down in a long time. You need to do something about it.'

'Ally doesn't want a life of constant upheaval,' Dev said as they made their way into the store. The chill of the air made him shiver; this was a world away from Kerala. 'I can't drag her around the world on my whims.'

'Is that what she told you? That she doesn't want adventure? Or are you still telling yourself you can't stop and settle down?' His brother's voice was gentle, almost coaxing.

'She has her life, her responsibilities in England.'

'So what's stopping you joining her there?'

'Bro, we were just messing around…until we weren't.'

To his surprise, his brother took his shoulders and stood in front of him, shaking him. 'Go to her. If she's not doing any more assignments with the NHF after this, she'll be home soon. Just go to her, Dev, and be honest this time.'

Dev flinched, as if the words 'be honest this time' were a blow. Romesh had a point. They paid for the beers and wine and walked to the car again in silence, but as the snowflakes started to swirl around the car, he couldn't help thinking he'd made the greatest mistake of his life, not being honest in the first place. He'd lost her trust, most of all, on top of the one person he would have talked to about this most, if she'd been here. Roisin. Squeezing his eyes shut, he pressed his back against the car door and fought a wall of emotions. Romesh was there in a flash. He held him tight as the grief overwhelmed him. 'I miss her so much, bro.'

'Roisin?'

'Yes, Roisin!'

'We all do, Dev, but you can't bring her back, no matter how much you keep chasing this impossible salvation. You can get Ally back, though, if you want.'

'Maybe.' Dev swallowed hard. 'It's just… there's so much to do out there.'

'And your work is the most honourable of anyone I know, the way you go wherever you're needed,' Romesh said, squeezing his shoulder a little too hard. 'But don't forget to help yourself too, Dev. Don't let this fear and grief dictate your life. You deserve more. Maybe if you give her a chance you can figure something out.'

Dev nodded, then pulled a face. 'That's what she said, but I lied to her. I told her I didn't have feelings for her when—' Dev broke off, the admission sticking in his throat. 'When I did. And I still do.'

'Then go to her, man,' his brother urged, his deep brown eyes shining with the same earnestness that reminded him of Roisin. 'Tell her how you feel.'

Ally lingered on the path to her house, her shopping bag swaying at her hip. She'd found Oliver's favourite chicken nuggets, he'd be pleased, and these days she lived for little victories. A hint of lavender from the garden next door hit her nose amongst the smell of the rain-soaked Somerset soil, and she stopped for a moment, letting the early March weather ground her in the present moment. This was where she was now. Back where she belonged in sweat-free Somerset, with the people who needed her. So why did she feel like a stranger impersonating her own life?

Shoving the vision of Dev from her head for the thousandth time that day, she was making her way up the driveway when she stopped short. A man she had never seen before was stepping out of her front door, onto the front step, pulling it closed behind him. Tall, dark hair, a loose denim jacket. He blinked in surprise when she met him halfway.

'Can I help you?' she asked, suspicion clear in her voice. For a moment he looked her up and down, and she clutched her shopping bag tighter, before he let out a laugh.

'You look just like her! She said that was the case. I'm Tim.'

He held out a hand and she stared at it, wracking her brains. Tim?

He must realise she had no clue who he was, because he retracted his hand slowly and dashed it awkwardly across his chin. 'Nora's friend,' he finished.

Ally drew a breath so sharp she almost sucked in the whole front garden. Nora had a new 'friend'? In what world…? Why had she not said anything? Ally had been home for almost a week!

'I um… I think you need to talk to your sister. Maybe I'll see you later. It's nice to finally meet you, Ally.'

She watched Tim walk away, his steps brisk and purposeful. She couldn't deny it, there was something rather likeable about him. Cute too. And there was also something about the way he carried himself that reminded her of Dev. She shook her head, banishing the thought. Dev was a million miles and a zillion emotions away, and there was no use dwelling on what could have been. That was what she'd been telling herself anyway, since she'd finished her last assignment and flown home. The emptiness was unparalleled, the feeling of rejection, and hurt, and stupidity for putting her heart on the line only to get it thrown back in her face. At least she'd told him though. At least she knew she was capáble of doing things on her own, facing some of those fears she'd let control her life since Matt.

Stepping inside the familiar house, she set down her bag on the dining table, trying to shake off the odd sense of disquiet Tim had just caused.

'Ally?' It was Nora's voice, calling from the other room.

'In here!' Ally called back, mustering a smile.

Nora looked sheepish as she stepped through the doorway. 'I saw you through the window just now. I see you met Tim?'

'Aunt Ally!' Oliver's voice rang out before she could reply. He dashed across the room, his arms flung wide. She bent down just in time to catch him, lifting him into a tight embrace. His joy was infectious, and, for a moment, she forgot about this new Tim guy. Ally's life was here, in Frome, amongst the people and the places that needed her. But still, Dev wouldn't leave her head. Neither would all the people she had met with the NHF, all the things they'd done. A world away from all this.

'Guess what?' Oliver's voice was a conspiratorial whisper against her ear now.

'What?' Ally played along, squeezing him gently.

'Mummy has a new boyfriend!'

The news struck her like a bucket of cold water.
So, Oliver knew too. That could only mean it was
serious. She sent her nephew to the kitchen with
the shopping bag, and looked up to find Nora
leaning against the back of the couch, the same
sheepish smile playing on her lips. Nora twid-
dled with the brown ponytail that hung over her
shoulder, and it was only now that Ally saw the
sparkle in her eyes. It hadn't been there in a very
long time.

Nora explained how they'd met, shortly before Ally had left for India, how the relationship had developed into something more, that she
couldn't have fought it even if she'd tried. How
Oliver seemed to adore him. She hadn't wanted
to tell her, she said, because she'd been so upset
about Dev.

Ally felt the swell of emotions almost topple
her. She was genuinely happy for Nora, delighted,
in fact, to see her sister taking steps towards happiness again. But beneath the surface, a million
more questions were bubbling up. 'Come sit,'
Nora said, gesturing to the kitchen table. 'We
need to talk. This guy in India… Canada, wherever…'

Ally watched as Nora folded her hands together, the lines of worry on her forehead smoothing out as she spoke. 'Ally, you've done so much

for us, for Oliver and me. But it's time you started thinking about yourself again.'

'Thinking about myself?' Ally echoed, her heart thudding a little harder. She could sense where this conversation was heading.

'Yes,' Nora continued, her tone gentle but firm. 'You should call the NHF. Take another assignment. Live your life.'

Ally felt a pang of longing just hearing mention of the NHF and the work she had left behind. The *man* she had left behind. He didn't want her, but she wanted more for herself these days. The warm monsoon rains, the laughter of all those children, and everything they had to teach her. For a fleeting second, she let herself imagine returning to that world, throwing herself head first into all the challenges and total fulfilment it had offered her, and potentially still could.

Larissa was happy, it seemed. She'd found a perfect match in her Thor in the end, and was talking about moving there to live in his cabin, and learn to shoot guns! Of all the crazy things her friend could do, this was pretty much the craziest. Nothing was the same around here now, and it probably never would be. Maybe the only way forward was to venture back out on her own.

Being in the old English pub was like stepping back in time, and somehow just as he'd imag-

ined as Dev took a wonky wooden seat at the bar.
The walls were lined with more weathered wood,
and the faint scent of ale from at least twenty de-
cades stung his nose along with the bleach. The
dim lighting cast shadows over an assortment of
tables where locals murmured over pints, their
laughter occasionally bubbling through the low
hum of conversation.

'Can I help you?' The barman, a grizzled man
with a salt-and-pepper beard, wiped his hands on
a cloth as he eyed Dev's out-of-place attire, and
the suitcase he'd wheeled in with him.

'Uh, yes,' Dev started. 'I'm looking for Ally
Spencer. Could you...could you call her for me? I
don't actually know where she lives. I'm a friend.
Her sister is Nora, if you know—'

'I know them. Sure thing,' the barman replied
with a nod, reaching for the phone behind the
counter.

As he waited, Dev's gaze wandered across the
quaint pub, right in the heart of Frome. It was
charming in its antiquity, and very different from
anything in Toronto. His stomach knotted at the
thought that maybe it was him, not this small
place, that Ally needed space from now. Would
she even hear him out if he found her?

Soon, though, the door swung open, pulling
Dev's attention towards it sharply. Ally's figure
appeared, framed by the doorway. Her wavy au-

burn hair tumbled around her shoulders, her eyes wide with disbelief as her gaze fell on him. He stood up quickly.

'Dev?' Her voice was barely audible over the clinking of glasses and chatter, though everyone stopped immediately to stare. This was probably the most exciting thing to have happened here in a long time.

'Nora told me someone was here to see me,' she stuttered, still in total shock. She paused half-way towards him, looking around her, as if expecting him to disappear again at any minute.

'Ally,' he breathed out in relief. He stepped towards her. 'I had to see you. I've been beating myself up over how I ended things.'

'So you…you came to Somerset?' She looked too shocked to laugh, or cry. In this moment he couldn't actually tell how she was feeling, but the distance between them was charging with electricity already. Dev felt his resolve harden; he was here now, and his family had all been rooting for him to do this, so he was not going to let them down. Thankfully she let him take her hands. She was dressed in jeans and boots, and a light jacket, so different from her array of summer dresses and NHF white coat. This was English Ally, and she was even more beautiful than he remembered.

His fingers brushed against hers as he reclaimed the space between them. 'I've been doing a lot of thinking, you know? About us, about myself.' He paused, searching her face for any sign of what she might be feeling. 'I shouldn't have lied to you. I will always regret the way I hurt you because of my own issues.'

Ally frowned, looking down at their entwined fingers. 'Did you talk with your family?'

'A lot.' He nodded sagely. 'It helped. *You* helped.'

She kept her eyes fixed on his, listening intently as he explained everything, all the love and support he had found the second he'd gone home and given them all a chance to open up, talk, and grieve together. A little vulnerability had infinitely changed the course of his life, and Ally had pushed him to make those changes. This new peace of mind was down to her, but she was still the missing piece he needed.

'I don't expect things to go back to how they were, but…' Dev hesitated, choosing his words with care. 'I understand if Frome is where you need to be. Maybe we can make it work. I mean, I've been offered work here before, and this place is kind of…interesting from what I've seen so far.'

Ally's expression softened, and she pulled her bottom lip between her teeth. The silence stretched, but it wasn't heavy; it was thoughtful, contemplative, and something lifted inside him.

'Actually, there's been a few changes around here, too,' she admitted at last, her gaze dropping to their hands before meeting his again. 'Nora... she's doing OK, and she wants me to, well, to live my life. She doesn't need me any more, really, not to the extent that she did. I think maybe it's me who needs her.'

Dev watched as Ally straightened her shoulders. He wanted to kiss her so badly, but people were still looking on. He ushered her to the corner, where he found his hands reaching for her, too. He pressed his lips to her warm forehead and felt her sigh, before she reached her arms up around his neck.

'I've been considering taking more assignments with the NHF,' she told him.

He pulled back, searched her face. 'Really?'

'I loved it. More than I thought, with or without you, believe it or not.'

Dev couldn't fight the laugh bubbling up his throat and out of his mouth. 'I can believe that. That sounds incredible, Ally.'

He meant it. She had come a long way, they both had, and for them to be here now together proved it. This was literally the last place on earth he'd expected to find himself, following an emotional reconnection with his family.

'Ally,' he began, the words tumbling out like a confession he'd been holding in since he'd abandoned her in that cloakroom, 'I've spent so much time running around that I forgot what it was like to feel… I don't know, anchored.' He paused, searching her eyes and finding the understanding he'd been praying for the whole way here on the plane.

She smiled. 'We don't have to be anchored though, Dev. We can go anywhere together first.'

'I want my next adventure to be different, with you.'

'So do I.' Her hand in his gave a reassuring squeeze, but Dev couldn't contain himself now. He brought his mouth to hers and kissed her, and the roar of the crowd in the pub made them both laugh so much they had to stop. Ally was flushed, and so was he, probably.

'I love you. And not just the idea of you, or the thrill of the chase. I love the real you. Of course, I almost told you the day of the quake, and of course, I just freaked out, and lied…'

Tears brimmed in her eyes. It had always been a gamble, laying his heart bare after everything, but the look she gave him now told him it had been worth the risk. And the expensive flight.

'Dev, I…' Ally's voice broke, and she took a moment to compose herself. 'I do love you too. You've flown halfway across the world to tell me that, to show me that you're serious about us.' She kissed him again, and took his hands in hers. 'There is just one thing we really have to do though,' she said, swiping at her damp eyes.

'And what is that?'

'We have to tell Nora that you're staying with us for now. There's more to Somerset than this pub, you know.'

'Well, I've a feeling I have the best tour guide in town,' Dev said, feeling the corners of his eyes crinkling as he smiled. 'Unless your man Oliver wants to show me around?'

Ally laughed, and grabbed the handle of his suitcase. 'Let's go and ask him, shall we?'

Fifteen months later

The doors swung open, and Ally stepped into the hall. She was a bundle of nerves, clutching the bouquet of roses to her gown, but the venue was alive with the soft glow of twinkling lights woven through the rafters, casting warm, dancing patterns on the guests, who turned to gaze at the brides. There was so much love in this room.

Larissa grinned at her from beside her. Her dark curls were bouncy as ever, adorned with tiny white flowers that matched the details of her wedding dress, and Ally felt the click of a hundred phone cameras on them, capturing this moment. Their joint wedding day!

'I still can't believe we're getting married,' Ally whispered in awe, but Larry's eyes were on

Erik now, waiting for her at the end of the aisle. He looked just as handsome as Dev, who found Ally's gaze and held it, anchoring her. They both looked the picture of a dashing, sexy groom in their navy-blue suits and ties, and as she found Dev's family in the crowd, sitting amongst their own, Ally knew she would always be grateful that people had flown from near and far to be here, in Somerset. Some of them had been surprised, considering the two couples no longer lived here, but home would always be home for her and Larissa.

The scent of roses and lilies hung in the air, stronger than the cow manure from the nearby field, for once, and she breathed in the subtle scent of beeswax from the candles. In the third row of seats she spotted Oliver whispering something to Dev's nephew, Nikki. Nora gave an eye roll and a shrug, which almost made Ally giggle into her bouquet. The kids were besties already. Last night, when they'd gathered in the meadow out back for a hog roast in the marquee, their families had all met properly, and they were like one big happy, crazy united bunch already. Even the ones from Svalbard seemed to be having a great time, not wearing a thousand layers of clothing for once. Early summer in Frome was delightfully…and quite surprisingly…warm.

'We are going to make the best wives in the

world,' Larry told her now, almost as if she was trying to convince herself as much as Ally. 'Even if our husbands hate *Bake Off*.'

'*We* can still watch it together, on Zoom calls,' she whispered back, and they both had to stop their giggles. Larissa was moving to a cabin in the middle of the Arctic Circle, after all. But her friend had fallen in love with Svalbard and the people too, and it seemed as if they'd fallen in love with her. Who wouldn't? The thought of visiting her there soon and seeing the life Larissa had built with Erik and their dogs filled Ally with the kind of happiness she'd never dreamed she would ever find again.

She and Dev hadn't managed to visit them yet, seeing as they'd been travelling through Cambodia and North Korea on their NHF assignments, but they'd vowed to meet at home at least every six months, and visit one another abroad when they could. Maybe they'd even all meet for Christmas in Toronto; there was still a lot to plan. At least Larry knew how to fire a gun and wouldn't wind up getting eaten by a polar bear before Ally got to visit Svalbard, she thought, suppressing another giggle.

Both women wore stunning white dresses. Nora had helped her choose hers, while Tim had taken Oliver to the toy store to pick out a board game. Ally's gown hugged her figure, the exact fit she knew would make Dev look at her in the way that melted her from the inside out. Larissa's was equally elegant and strapless, and made her boobs look phenomenal.

The brush of her dress against the polished wooden floor grounded her as her eyes found Dev standing tall and looking at her so proudly it sent a lump to her throat. His gaze locked on hers again with a love so tangible it felt as though he were reaching out and enveloping her in his big arms. He took her hands as she took her place opposite him, just as Larry stopped before Erik.

You look beautiful, Dev mouthed, and she sniffed back a tear. Getting married, saying her vows next to her best friend, and knowing she would spend the rest of her adventurous life with the man of her dreams was almost too much, let alone the fact that they were starting this journey here—in this place!

It was hard to imagine that this hall used to be their clinic. The operation had moved to another town and the clinic space had been sold and reopened as a refitted event space she had sworn never to visit, but she and Larry had both been enchanted by it the second they'd stepped inside, just on the off chance that the perfect Somerset venue they'd been searching for could be this one. And what a way to celebrate their friendship, too. This was something they'd remember for ever, both marrying their partners in the very place where they had first become friends.

'Ready?' Larissa whispered now, squeezing Ally's hand.

'Ready if you are,' she answered with a smile.

* * * * *

If you missed the previous story in the Valentine Flings duet, then check out
Hot Nights with the Arctic Doc
by Luana DaRosa

*And if you enjoyed this story,
check out these other great reads
from Becky Wicks*

Tempted by the Outback Vet
Daring to Fall for the Single Dad
A Marriage Healed in Hawaii

All available now!

HARLEQUIN
Reader Service

Enjoyed your book?

Try the perfect subscription for Romance readers and get more great books like this delivered right to your door.

See why over 10+ million readers have tried Harlequin Reader Service.

Start with a Free Welcome Collection with free books and a gift—valued over $20.

Choose any series in print or ebook. See website for details and order today:

TryReaderService.com/subscriptions